escaping indigo
BOOK TWO

skin hunger

ELI LANG

Riptide Publishing
PO Box 1537
Burnsville, NC 28714
www.riptidepublishing.com

Cover art: Natasha Snow, natashasnowdesigns.com
Editor: May Peterson
Layout: L.C. Chase, lcchase.com/design.htm

ISBN: 978-1-62649-618-7

First edition
November, 2017

Also available in ebook:
ISBN: 978-1-62649-617-0

escaping indigo
BOOK TWO

skin hunger

ELI LANG

For my grandmothers.
And for LL. Live as you like.

TABLE OF contents

chapter one

I clenched my hand on the armrest. The fabric was rough and nubby beneath my palm, but thin enough that I briefly wondered if I'd tear it. There wasn't even anything to be afraid of, and I kept trying to tell myself that, to use logic to get rid of the anxiety. But fear was an illogical thing. And squeezing an armrest to death would have more of an immediate effect on my fear than any reasoning ever would.

I thought about closing my eyes and pretending I was somewhere else, but I figured that would make it easier for me to picture something going horribly wrong. Better if I could see. At least it would give me the illusion of some control. I took a deep breath and wished, futilely and not for the first time that day, that I wasn't alone. That Tuck, my best friend and the guitar player for our band, was here next to me, cracking jokes in an attempt to distract me. That Bellamy, our singer, and his boyfriend, Micah, were sitting in the seats in front of me, Bellamy's voice drifting back while he worried about our instruments and equipment being handled correctly by the airline. I even missed Quinn, our sort-of manager, and his perpetual, overbearing protectiveness.

But instead I was by myself, flying somewhere I didn't want to go, and scared before we'd even gotten off the ground.

I sighed and leaned my head back against the seat. Passengers were slowly making their way down the aisle still, bumping elbows and knees with bags that looked like they would never fit in the overhead compartments. No one had claimed either of the seats next to me yet—I'd snagged the window seat for myself, so I could see what was happening—and I hoped no one would. It'd be nice to stretch out, sleep a little, so that I wouldn't be quite so groggy when we landed in the morning.

I changed my mind when a tall girl stopped at my row and casually hoisted her bag into the overhead compartment. She glanced down at me after she closed the latch, and smiled before she slid into the aisle seat.

I was staring, and probably being obvious enough that she'd notice, but I couldn't stop. She wasn't particularly striking. She wasn't an average beauty queen. Her dark-blond hair was cut too short for that. It fluttered around her ears and her bangs drifted into her eyes. The length of it made her face appear almost too long, but not quite. Her makeup was heavy, dark, but it suited her, brought out the green in her eyes. There was something about the way she carried herself, though, that made me want to watch her move. She had an almost tomboy style going on, but she was elegant, graceful. She'd lifted her bag overhead like it was nothing, the slender lines of her wrists and arms delicate in their strength. Now she buckled her seat belt with the same smooth movement, her shoulders straight, fingers careful on the metal and cloth. Then she turned back to me. I was still staring, my brain screaming at me to look away. She brushed the hair out of her face with a flick of her finger, and I realized I must have been wrong before. They weren't green, but blue—almost too pale but absolutely lovely.

"Hi," I said stupidly. God, I couldn't remember the last time this had happened to me, the last time I'd been completely stuck for words. I was objective. I didn't get swoony over every attractive person I saw. Maybe it was because we were going to be stuck on an airplane together for six hours, but after that, we'd go our separate ways. Safe, or as near to safe as you could get.

She smiled back shyly. "Hi."

Her voice was soft and sort of husky. She twisted toward me a bit in her seat, and the olive-green jacket she was wearing fell into perfect place. Even her clothes wanted to do the graceful thing. It was captivating. I hadn't seen anything quite like her before.

Then I realized I wasn't just staring, I was *staring,* and it was totally inappropriate and probably creeping her out. I wanted to say something, make that banal conversation you normally would when you were stuck next to a stranger, but I was too tired, my brain fried from the last few weeks of touring. Maybe it wouldn't have helped anyway. Maybe she already thought I was a psycho with no self-control. I gave her a little nod instead, turned to gaze out the window, and tried to pretend that I wasn't on the plane and this lovely girl wasn't sitting two seats away.

My small show of boredom and indifference lasted right up until we were cruising down the runway. Everything was fine, fine, and I kept repeating that to myself like I could make the irrational part of my mind believe it. But when the plane tilted up, leaving the ground in that sudden way, letting loose that disturbing feeling of being completely untethered, I gasped. I had to keep staring out the window. If we were going to crash, I—perversely—wanted to see it coming. There was that idiotic imaginary control again, the idea that if I watched closely enough, nothing bad could happen. Or, if it did happen, I'd be able to do something about it.

A warm hand covered mine, thin fingers squeezing down, and any thoughts of watching for a crash flew right out of my head. I flinched and turned to the girl. She had her arm stretched out, and she was leaning over her own armrest so she could touch me.

"Are you okay?"

I nodded, but I didn't know what to say. My mouth was totally dry, with nerves from a host of different sources.

She gave me that same tiny smile as before, but this time it seemed more thoughtful than shy. "Sorry." She started to move her hand away, moving back over the space that separated us. "You looked—"

The plane tilted the other way, and my heart leaped up until it was lodged somewhere just behind my tongue. I flipped my hand over, the movement desperate and completely unconscious, and grabbed at her retreating fingers. For a second, I felt the hesitation in her, the tension in her arm, as if she were trying to decide whether to pull away or not. But it was only for a moment, a short one. Then she did move, but it was to lean closer and to wrap her fingers around mine.

After another minute, the plane straightened out, and I could breathe more easily. I looked up at the girl. She was watching me, watching while I took deep breaths and tried to calm down, to slow my heartbeat, and when I met her eyes, I was embarrassed.

My palm was sweaty and sticky against hers, and I knew I must look like a complete fool, panicking when no one else was, when there was absolutely nothing to be afraid of. I couldn't help the fear, and I accepted it. Normally I was okay with it, because it was something that wasn't pleasant or easy but simply *was*, and I could deal with that. But I didn't want this girl to see me like that. I didn't want to imagine anyone had seen me like that, but especially her, right now.

I drew in another shaky breath. She still had a hold of my hand, and as much as I wanted to wipe my palm on my jeans, I didn't want to let go either. I raised my other hand and brushed my bangs out of my face.

"I don't like flying," I said. Captain Obvious. Great.

Her smile went a little wider, and I thought I might hear some teasing, but there was none. She pressed her fingers to mine. Our wrists nearly lined up, and I imagined I could feel the steady pulse in hers, counterpoint to the erratic leaping of mine. She held my hand until the plane had stopped twisting in the sky and we were more or less steady, and I wasn't flinching at every move. Then she let me go, carefully untangling our fingers. She was even polite enough not to wipe her palm off once our hands had separated.

"Thanks." My voice still sounded tight, but I'd probably be okay, now that we'd gotten past the takeoff stage and the plane was even, and I could almost, almost imagine I was on a bus instead, cruising down the highway, firmly on the ground.

She nodded. "Sure." She hesitated, then reached her hand back out for me to shake. "I'm Cara."

"Ava."

She sat back in her seat and gazed at me, studying me almost like I'd studied her before. She had a book in her lap, but she hadn't opened it yet. Her fingers brushed over the cover.

"Ava. What's making you take a red-eye all the way across the country?"

I laughed, short and soft. Around us, the cabin lights were dimming, and there was the shifting, rustling noise of people trying to get comfortable enough to sleep in a cramped space. "You mean I don't look like someone who might travel to see the fall foliage?"

She grinned back and shook her head. "Nope. And it's too early for it to be any good yet, anyway. But you don't have to say," she added hastily. "Sorry. I'm used to talking to people, but I shouldn't have pried."

My turn to shake my head. "Nah, it's fine. I'm going . . ." I almost said *home*, but the word caught in my throat. Where I was headed wasn't home. Home was the place I'd left a few hours ago, the people I'd left. I wasn't sure when it had happened. Even when I'd been so eager to leave my parents' place, the town I'd grown up in, when I'd finally escaped to a college across the country, I'd always called where I was from *home*. But somewhere along the way, that had shifted. I didn't think of it that way anymore.

"I'm visiting family," I said. "Annual trip." Or it would have been, if my parents had had their way. I'd put it off the last two years in a row. Maybe three, if I bothered to count. I'd begged off with a crazy touring and recording schedule, and made do with seeing my parents, and maybe my cousin, briefly whenever Escaping Indigo passed through. I hadn't actually gone there on purpose, to spend any time there, in years. "My grandmother's going into assisted living too. So I'm going to help." It was the only reason I'd been corralled into a trip this long. I'd had to do it.

Cara nodded.

"You?" I asked, because I was curious, and because I wanted to stop talking about myself and why I was going. I didn't want to think about it. If I did, I'd start thinking about how I'd wanted to get off the plane as soon as I'd gotten on, how I wanted to turn around and get back to my friends and the place I belonged.

She smiled. "Going home. I went out for a dance thing."

"Oh." What I knew about dance could fit in a tissue. My mother had tried to make me go when I was younger. It was the thing all little girls were supposed to do, and I probably had gone a few times, but it hadn't lasted, and I couldn't remember much about it. It was never going to be my thing, and I'd put it behind me like all the other things my parents had pushed at me. "That's really cool," I told Cara now. It was, and I thought I should say more, but didn't know what else wouldn't sound completely ignorant, either.

I wanted to ask her more about it, but a huge yawn caught me. I covered my mouth, embarrassed, but Cara smiled and shook her head. "You look exhausted."

I huffed out a laugh. Maybe I should be taking that as an insult, but I couldn't quite. "It's been a crazy couple of weeks." Touring always was. This round had actually been easier, calmer, than any tours I could remember before. We'd finally kind of *made it*. We had a tour bus and enough money in our pockets that we knew we weren't going to starve, cash to pay people to help us while we traveled so we didn't have to do every little thing ourselves, and while the venues we played weren't massive, I wasn't quite as worried that we were all going to be ax murdered in a back alley because the place was so scuzzy. It wasn't like those early days, when Tuck and Bellamy and I had lived out of a van for weeks on end, sleeping with our gear so we wouldn't get ripped off, playing for crowds who weren't always exactly sure who we were. Happy when we were making enough money to pay for gas so we could get to the next city. I was glad those days were over.

Sometimes I missed the simplicity in them, though, missed how each day was only about putting one foot in front of the other, and nothing else. That was all there had been—a steady march toward our goal—and it had made everything so clear, had given me so much focus. Now it was easier but also somehow so much more complicated. We'd arrived, we'd actually gotten to where we'd wanted to go, and there were possibilities and options spread out before us, so that sometimes they seemed endless, and that wasn't anything but good. But it was scary too, and it made me want to sleep forever sometimes, so I wouldn't have to stare those big things in the face.

"Why don't you stretch out?" Cara asked.

My mind, not really performing at peak, went in about a million directions, and half of them were dirty. I was immediately embarrassed with myself. Cara's smile twisted slightly to the side, and I knew that whatever I was thinking was showing clear on my face, or clear enough for her to at least get some idea of it. Doubly so now, probably—a blush spread over my cheeks and up my neck. I didn't blush cute. I blushed in splotches and spots, uneven patches of red that were as embarrassing as whatever was causing them. I sighed, but Cara reached out before I could look away or say anything, and ran her hand down my arm. It was only a couple of inches, elbow to forearm, but it was enough to make me shiver, to make me want to lean in to that touch. I hadn't expected that reaction from myself, but it had been a long time since anyone had touched me quite like that—tender and gentle and a little bit shy—touched me to bring me back to them. I couldn't even remember when the last time had been.

She raised the armrest on her seat and patted the cushion of the seat between us. "My schedule's all messed up. I don't think I'm going to be able to sleep. But you could." A slight blush, the faintest pink, spread across her own cheekbones. "If you want."

What I wanted, with something that felt almost like surprise, was to stay awake and keep flirting with this girl. Even though I was pretty obviously doing a terrible job of flirting. It had been so long since I'd had any practice, and it was showing. I kept putting my foot in my mouth. Maybe it would be best to stop while I was ahead. And I *was* tired, anyway. I hadn't been kidding when I'd told Cara that it had been a long few weeks. Good weeks, but draining nonetheless. And this would be my last chance to simply . . . sleep and rest and not think about where I was coming from or where I was going. Caught safe in the middle while we were in the air, before we landed and I had to deal with my family and being back in my hometown and everything that meant.

I nodded. "Thank you. That would . . . That would be really good."

She nodded back and moved her hand for me, freeing the space. I lifted my own armrest and curled over onto my side, squashing my jacket under my head for a makeshift pillow. It wasn't exactly comfortable. It was too tight and the seats were too narrow, so my knees hung over the edge. But I'd slept in worse positions. It was more space than I would have had otherwise, and I didn't care if it wasn't exactly ideal.

I was careful not to let my head touch Cara's leg. She'd been the one to suggest the whole thing, but that didn't mean I could push into her personal space any more than I already had. For a second, I worried about drooling or snoring in my sleep, and how mortifying that would be. But then my eyes were closing, the long day finally getting the best of me, and any worries I had faded away as I drifted off.

I woke up with a start to turbulence and the place bouncing underneath me. I clutched at the seat, disoriented from sleep and the weirdness of realizing I was traveling through the air. I wondered if I should sit up, but my bleary mind was telling me I should figure out what was going on first and try to decide if I needed to panic.

A hand landed on my shoulder and squeezed, gentle but firm, grounding. "Nothing to worry about." Cara's voice was soft and low. I woke up some more, glanced around. The plane was quiet, the lights all dimmed except for the tiny strips of gold that outlined the center aisle. Outside the windows, the sky was black, only the lightest spatter of stars visible. I took a deep breath and tried to orient myself, remind myself that it was fine.

"Some bumpy weather," Cara said. "That's all it is. No big deal."

I nodded and briefly considered trying to go back to sleep, but I didn't think I could. I must have been out for a while anyway. I sat up slowly, and something slid off my shoulders into my lap. I caught it before it fell to the floor and saw that it was a gray hoodie, fleece lined and warm. Something I'd wear, but it wasn't mine. I handed it back to Cara. "Thanks."

She shrugged. "You looked cold."

I smiled at her. I was grateful. It seemed to me that small gestures like that were sometimes the hardest to do, but they were the sweetest. It definitely felt sweet to me, and I wanted to sit here and savor it. But it reminded me of Tuck too, of all the thoughtful but nearly mindless ways he took care of me, the habits we had between us that were so ingrained in us that we didn't even have to think about them anymore. Making sure we were comfortable, always being there to make lunch because we knew the other would forget to eat otherwise, being someone to call because we always knew when we needed someone to reach out to. To cover the other while we were napping. That was Tuck for me, and me for him. Except it was different now, so different, and that had been so painfully obvious on this last tour. I loved that Cara had given me her hoodie. I wanted to take it in the lightness and kindness with which it was meant. I wanted it to be simple. My mind was just making everything so goddamned complicated.

I tried to shove all of that back. When I was nervous, or awkward, or unsure, I tried to remember that I was, technically, a rock star.

As technically as you could define that label, anyway. And although I definitely didn't think that made me any better than anyone else, I could pull that persona on like my own soft, fuzzy hoodie when I needed it, and let it keep me safe. Let it carry me, at least for a while. I tried to do that now, tried to remember that if I could be confident enough to get up on stage in front of thousands of people, I could damn well carry on a conversation. I grabbed for something to say, something to break the awkwardness that was growing between us, but I couldn't think of anything.

"Why dance?" I asked finally, because that had been interesting, and it was the only thing I could think of.

Cara looked surprised with my abrupt shot at conversation, but she let it go. She leaned toward me, over the seat that separated us, and I leaned in too. Her voice was quiet when she started talking, likely so we wouldn't wake anyone around us. "I don't know. I wanted to move, I think. I had a lot of energy when I was a kid. My mom thought it would be a good idea, something for me to try. And I was good at it."

It was a simple answer, but she seemed like she was actually considering it, like maybe if I gave her enough time, she'd tell me even more. I wondered if she'd have answered that way if we weren't in this confined space, in the dark, amidst the warm, soft sounds of people sleeping. It felt intimate, suffocating and magical at the same time, in the oddest way.

"Do you like it?" I asked, because liking it hadn't really come into her answer.

She opened her mouth, then closed it and tilted her head in something that was almost a shake or a nod, but not quite either. "It's kind of like being in love," she said after a minute. She blushed right away, enough that I could see it, even in the dark.

And yeah, it was a silly thing to say. But I thought maybe I fell a bit in love with her right then, because she *had* said it. In this weird pocket of intimacy, it seemed particularly secret and special. Even though we were strangers and would go our separate ways, so it didn't matter what we said to each other. People didn't say that kind of thing. I nodded, keeping my expression serious, so she'd know I wasn't laughing, and she continued.

"When you're in love, you're, like . . . blissful and crazy and angry and it's awesome, but it's tiring and awful too. But you don't want to stop being in love." She laughed and pushed her hair out of her eyes. "That sounds crazy. Sorry."

I shook my head, was shaking it even before she finished talking. "No, it doesn't, not at all. That sounds . . . about exactly right."

She laughed, just a puff of air escaping her lips. "Yeah? What do you do, then? Something that makes you feel like being in love?"

I pulled in a breath and nodded. She had no idea how close being in love was to what I did. "I'm a drummer in a rock band." It still felt weird for me to be able to say that and have it be the first and last truth about my life, the rock I built everything else on. It was all I had wanted, all I had gone after for so long. For so many years, when it had been exactly as wonderful and awful as being in love, when it had seemed like it was impossible and would never happen, no matter how hard we tried. But now it had, and it felt surreal and better than wonderful.

Didn't stop people from giving me some serious side-eye when I pulled that out as my career, though.

Cara didn't, quite. Maybe because she made dance her career, so she was used to doing things that were a little different than what people expected.

"Why drums?" she asked, throwing my own question back at me. It didn't feel like a challenge, though, or not exactly like one. It felt like the same curiosity I'd had.

I shrugged. "It was all I ever wanted. It fit for me." The words just spilled out, but I figured that was as close to the truth as I could come without talking and talking, so I left it there.

Cara nodded. "So you *do* know what I mean."

I laughed. "Yeah. I do."

"And you're . . ." She grinned, and I thought I saw the blush come back. "You make a living doing that?"

I raised an eyebrow. "You make a living dancing?" I wondered what type of dance she did. Ballet? Did she wear one of those frilly outfits?

"Sorry." She glanced down. "Shouldn't have asked like that. But yes, I do."

I waved my hand between us. "It's fine. And yeah, I do too. Sometimes we even get played on the radio."

"Oh yeah?" She leaned slightly closer. "Have I heard of you?"

I hated this part. I was never sure what answer I wanted from someone when I told them my band was Escaping Indigo. If they knew us, that was awesome, and I was so pleased that we could actually be recognized by name. But they always had an opinion, and whether it was good or bad, whether they kept it to themselves, it changed the way people saw me. And if, on the other hand, they didn't know who we were, then everybody was embarrassed.

I pointed down at my carry-on, tucked under my seat. I had a patch sewn onto it, with our band logo. It was probably pretentious to have it there, but I loved my band, and I liked the idea that people saw it and maybe wondered. And I wanted to be able to see our name, remind myself that it *was* real. Cara followed where I was pointing, and I could tell before she even looked back up at me, by the way she went still, that she was in the first camp of people, that she knew who we were.

She turned back to me, and I smiled, but I was nervous. She blinked and smiled too, but it looked as hesitant as mine felt. "I've heard of you." She sounded honestly surprised.

I wanted to be pleased, and a big part of me was. Awfully pleased. How many times in the past had people asked, and I'd said our band name, and they hadn't known we existed at all? It went more the other way these days, and that was definitely okay with me. "We do all right."

"I haven't heard a lot." She sounded apologetic. "I don't listen to the radio very often. But I liked what I did hear," she added, fast, leaning forward like she wanted to press that into me.

I laughed, and it wasn't an uncomfortable laugh, but a real one. Honesty I could deal with. "That's totally fine. Some of my best friends are in bands who make music I can't stand."

"I really did like it. I'm not telling you that to make you happy." She pulled her mouth down tight at the corners as she absorbed what else I had said. "Seriously? Do you tell them you don't like their stuff?"

I shook my head. Short pieces of hair were escaping my ponytail, getting in my eyes. I pulled the tie out and ran my fingers through my hair, hoping it wasn't as much of a disaster as it felt. "We don't talk about it. But no one's going to like everything. Doesn't mean I don't think they're great people."

She was staring at me, and I wondered if I'd said something weird. Then she laughed and pinched the bridge of her nose before she dropped her hand. She was still grinning at me, and I smiled in response, even though I didn't know why.

"That's . . . a really generous way to think."

"Nah. It's selfish. Lets me have more friends than I probably should."

Cara's smile went soft. "I'm glad you were the one I sat next to tonight, Ava."

"Yeah?" It occurred to me, for the first time, that I'd been flirting with Cara—to the best of my flirting abilities, which, admittedly weren't much, but still—this whole time, and I didn't even know if she was into other girls that way. But I thought my flirting had been pretty obvious . . . okay, maybe not the flirting itself, but the staring, probably, had tipped my hand. She hadn't stopped me, or rebuffed me, and now, as she watched me with that curious, half-timid look that you only gave someone you were interested in, I thought maybe she was. Maybe I had actually gotten lucky enough to sit next to a gorgeous, kind girl who might even find me attractive. And when we landed . . . what? Was I going to be bold and ask for her number, when I wasn't even going to be around for very long? I mentally shook my head at myself. *Flirt*, I told myself. *Have fun. Remember what it's like to be with someone who isn't a quick bang in a parking lot or a dressing room. And then call it done*. That was really all I could do here.

I still wanted to ask for her number as we were getting off the plane, though. We'd talked quietly for the rest of the flight, and it had been . . . easy. Yeah, there were still those awkward pauses that happened when two people didn't know each other. But it hadn't been enough to make us stop. The hum of our voices had surrounded us, made a pocket for us on the plane. Sometimes Cara would make a wry joke, and I'd laugh out loud, then have to cover my mouth to keep myself from waking everyone else. And I had liked it. It had felt so good to sit with her and . . . be absorbed in her and our conversation, for those few hours.

When we landed, the sun was just coming up, making the clouds we'd flown through pink and pearl gray. The sunlight in the airport was almost blinding, after all the darkness, the shadows of the airplane cabin. I rubbed at my eyes and hoisted my bag higher up on my shoulder. Ahead of me, Cara was already weaving her way through people, headed to baggage claim. We'd said goodbye on the plane, both of us saying how great it was to have met, but it had been more than pleasantries for me. It had been the truth—I really had been happy to sit next to her, and I thought maybe it had been the same for her. But I still didn't ask for her number, and she didn't ask for mine either.

I'd gotten to be an expert at packing a lot in a small bag and not carrying as much, since we'd started touring, so my carry-on was all I had. No reason to follow Cara any farther toward the baggage claim. I made my way toward the rental cars instead. The people at the counter looked me up and down when I got there, and I had to show my license to prove that I was over the twenty-five-year age limit. The little slip of plastic with my picture on it proved the truth—I was pushing thirty. Not very old, but I still didn't like telling people. I wasn't vain. I didn't buy into that bullshit about getting old. But rock stars had expiration dates. There was no getting around that. Everything had to be done so quickly, so you could fit yourself into that magic age slot. We tried to pretend it didn't happen, and if you actually ended up making it in music, that expiration date got pushed way back. But I didn't think any of us ever completely rid ourselves of the fear of being over twenty, over thirty. It was too ingrained.

I was still sneakily pleased when the rental people had to hand the car over to me.

The sun had come over the horizon by the time I started driving to my parents' house. It was low enough, however, that it was hitting the trees just right, gilding them in light, turning the greens gold and emerald, and making everything look so lush and gorgeous and perfect that it was hard to see any flaws, almost hard to remember that I hated it here. The leaves threw shadows on the car and the road, making the light flicker as I drove underneath. It was beautiful, but confining too, the forest bumping right up against the guardrails. I thought about turning on the radio, filling the silence in the car, but I half imagined that all that greenery and light would soak up the sound. We had trees back home, and our foliage was actually probably far more lush, the semi-tropical weather ensuring that even our weeds grew well. But it wasn't old growth like this. It didn't loom over you and feel like it might swallow you up in a swirl of summer colors. Even though I'd grown up here, I always forgot exactly what it was like, and I had to get used to it each time, all over again. And each time it took longer than it had the time before.

I drove back roads to my parents' house as much as I could. The streets were narrow and twisty, and squirrels kept darting out in front of me and stopping in the road, making me slam my brakes on. It seemed too closed in, too wild, to be a neighborhood, but houses, some set back, some sitting right on the road, were scattered every acre or two. An old neighborhood, with old houses to match. Low ceilings and decorative lintels. Moss growing up the clapboard and brick. They were pretty and tiny, cramped and quaint. I'd grown up in a house like these, with uneven floors and doors that stuck in their jambs, and a huge backyard with scruffy gardens along the edges. It had been an adventure, as a kid, had always felt comfortable and . . . like what my adult mind imagined home was supposed to be.

Apparently it hadn't been quite as much like a home to my parents, because they'd sold it right after I'd switched colleges and moved across the country. They still lived in the same town, but now their house was newer. Squished together with other houses, with a tiny, neatly trimmed lawn. Doors that opened silently on well-oiled hinges, jambs that hadn't been warped by time and damp. Floors that were shiny and even. Plumbing that didn't croak when you ran the water. Sterile in appearance and design, but neat and easy. Less maintenance. Cleaner. I got the appeal in that. I got wanting things to be easy.

Didn't mean I really liked the place, though.

I parked in the driveway, and my dad had the front door open before I even got out of the car. For a second, I stared at him through the windshield. It hadn't really been that long since I'd seen him, and he looked nearly the same, with his gray sweater-vest and his glasses perched on the end of his nose. Nerdy chic, I'd always called it in my mind. Or comfortable and warm. And I realized that I'd missed him, more than I'd expected, or allowed myself to think. I left my bag where it was and jogged up the short path to him. He opened his arms without a word and wrapped me up in a tight hug.

He pushed me a little bit away, holding my arms so he could study me. I was almost looking at him eye to eye. That always surprised me, that I was as tall as my dad, since I wasn't very tall myself. His glasses were slipping down his nose, and I reached up and pushed them back for him. He smiled at me.

"You look so tired."

I sighed and wondered if anyone was going to notice anything about me while I was here aside from my lack of sleep. "Not what a girl wants to hear."

"Not what anyone wants to hear," he replied, gently but still chastising. He'd always been able to do that, put me in place or drive home a point without ever raising his voice, without even really changing his tone.

"I'm fine."

He nodded, but he didn't say anything else. I figured that topic wasn't done, but he was letting it go for now. "Come inside."

I went back to the car and got my bag. My dad offered to carry it for me, and I let him, even though I spent my life toting around drums that weighed ten times what was in that bag.

He brought my carry-on inside and set it down by the door, and I stood in the foyer and gazed around. I had to give it to the house—it was *bright*. Our old house had been so surrounded by trees that it had been like living in a fishbowl, all shadows and watery light. But this place was filled with sun—airy and open and clean. My mom loved that about it, that she could actually see what she was doing, that she wasn't constantly fighting with a house that was older than she was.

Like I'd summoned her with the thought, she came around a corner and into sight. She walked toward me and held her arms out like my father had. She let me go quickly, and leaned back so she could stare at me, pushing my hair away from my eyes and taking me in. Making judgments about how I looked and what it meant. I knew she was. But she didn't say anything. I almost wished she would, so we could have it out of the way. The rest of me was glad for the momentary reprieve.

Breakfast was easier than I'd anticipated, and I realized that it was this very moment, when we all sat down together for the first time in so long and tried to make conversation, that I'd been dreading more than anything. I loved my parents, I really did, but there was a disconnect in the way we related to each other. They had always expected, wanted, me to be one thing, and I had always wanted to be something else. There was still a part of them, I knew, that wondered why I hadn't been what they'd imagined I would be. Why I hadn't finished college and done something normal and banal. Useful. I was different, in so many ways, than they had expected, and I didn't think they could understand quite how that had happened.

I didn't even want to imagine what the expressions on their faces would be if I told them about Cara. If I told them about how I'd met a girl I thought was beautiful, a girl who'd touched me in a way that I hadn't been touched in so long. A girl I wanted to kiss and hold and maybe be with, if things had been different and there had been any chance of that. I wasn't in the closet, exactly, but my sexuality wasn't something I talked about with many people, and my parents had never been on that short list.

But maybe I really did look too tired for anything more than a surface conversation, because they stuck to easy subjects. They filled me in on when my cousin was driving up, when dinner with my aunt would be, and what the schedule was for moving my grandmother into the assisted-living facility. Stuff that was simple and that we probably wouldn't end up at each other's throats over. Granted, I didn't ask how my gran was feeling about the whole leaving-her-house thing, and my parents didn't tell me. Maybe no one had asked her. Maybe they didn't want to ask because they knew she was bold enough to tell them exactly how she felt, and they could already guess. Maybe no one wanted to allow her to make it real.

I didn't really know what to do there. My grandmother and I had never been close. I didn't think my grandmother was disappointed with me the way my parents were. I thought she just hadn't ever known me, really. We hadn't taken the time or energy to know each other. It was like we existed on two different planes. But I was here, and I planned to help, and if that meant figuring out what was really going on in her mind about all of this, well, then I would do it.

Not right now, though. Not for these few brief minutes when my parents and I were getting along and sitting together at the same table and I could pretend this was a slice of my childhood, before I'd started defying everything they wanted from me.

After, I carried my bag upstairs and closed the door behind me in the guest room. I pulled my phone out of my pocket and flopped down on the bed. I wanted to sleep for hours, just lie here in this room that was completely unfamiliar. But I had people to see, plans to make. I'd have to get up, have a shower, get ready for the day. I could only take a few minutes here for myself, right now.

I sent a text to my cousin Zevi, telling him I'd meet him when he got to town, and asking when he was arriving. He didn't write back, and I figured he was still driving. Then I checked my own messages. I had two from Tuck—a story he'd heard, that was mostly funny because he was such a terrible storyteller. The next was him saying his girlfriend, Lissa, had reminded him to ask if I got in okay. I laughed at both of them, but then I let myself wallow in being alone. I felt so isolated here. Like I'd been sent to the other side of the planet and I was an alien. The idea of Tuck and Lissa talking about me, him thinking about me, made me feel, perversely, even more alone. I had to put the phone down on my chest, wrap my hand around it, and hide the screen from myself for a few minutes.

I had a message from Micah too, and when I picked the phone back up, I checked it. I hadn't known Micah long—he'd joined us as a roadie on the second-to-last tour, and he and Bellamy had become inseparable pretty quickly. I liked them together. I liked Micah. He was so *good*. He felt like a friend I'd known for a long time, instead of only a few months.

I called him, even though it would be stupidly early there, and even though I could have called Tuck or Bellamy or Quinn instead.

He answered on the third ring. His voice was a little gravelly, and I could tell he was trying to keep the sleep out of it.

"Did I wake you?" I tilted my head to the side so I could see out the window. There was a huge oak tree there, something that must have been there before construction had started on the neighborhood. They must have built around it. I'd had a tree like that outside my childhood bedroom too. When I was a teenager, I'd used it to escape, climbing down and sneaking across the backyard, leaving my window open a crack so I could sneak back. I wondered if I could do that with this tree too. Then I remembered that I wasn't a kid anymore, and if I wanted to go in or out late, I could use my key and the front door.

Micah cleared his throat. "Nah, I'm up. I'm making coffee. Bellamy's still asleep."

He yawned into the phone, and I wanted to laugh, but I found myself yawning too. He clinked something around—the coffee maker, maybe—and there was silence on the line for a second, but it wasn't weird. I liked listening to him being domestic, liked knowing he was taking care of Bellamy, and himself. I liked that they were back home, doing what they always did, their routine the same, even though I was all the way across the country and everything, right now, was different for me.

"You get in okay?" he asked when he'd gotten things settled.

I nodded, not caring that he couldn't see me. "I miss you," I blurted out. I could feel my face burning. I ought to give in and wear heavy blush all the time if this was going to keep up. I was just so glad to hear his voice.

He laughed, but it was gentle, like he wasn't quite laughing *at* me. "You've only been gone a day, Ava."

I sighed. "I know. But . . ." I lowered my voice. "I don't want to be here. I hate it."

There was a long pause, and I thought maybe I'd pushed it too far. When it came down to it, Micah and I didn't really know each other that well. It only felt like we did.

Then he said, "It can't be all bad. There must be something good you can tell me." And I realized he'd only been searching for the right thing to say.

"Is this one of your therapy things?" I didn't mean to sound so defensive. It just happened. I felt awful as soon as the words were out.

"Therapy's been good for me and Bellamy," Micah said quietly. Calm but firm, and I knew I'd hit a sore spot. "Not sure how much Bellamy actually likes it, but it's a step."

"I know. I'm sorry. I didn't mean it like that."

"I know. You convinced Bellamy to go in the first place, so . . ."

"No, that was all Bellamy." And it had been. I'd nudged him, because I'd wanted him to be happy, and I'd been heart sore at seeing him so sad, but we'd all wanted it to be his choice. I seriously believed it should be. And he'd done it. He'd gotten Micah to go too. I think that had surprised Micah—to think that, the entire time he was trying to get his boyfriend help, he could use help working out his own stuff in the same way.

Micah took a deep breath and what sounded like a sip of coffee. "Okay. So. Tell me."

My brain went in exactly one direction, and I decided to just say it. "I met a really awesome girl on the plane."

"Oh yeah? How awesome?"

I swallowed and lay back against the pillow. Cara's face filled my mind. Had she been as pretty, as graceful, as I remembered, really? I thought she had. But I didn't know how much of that to tell Micah. I'd never talked to him about this type of thing before.

Maybe that would make it easier. To pretend it was no big deal, because he was someone new in my life. Maybe it would be simpler.

"She was sweet. She let me sleep beside her, and then when I woke up, we talked for the rest of the flight." I took a deep breath. *What could it hurt?* I told myself. *How could it go wrong?* It shouldn't have been able to, but I was still nervous. I didn't want to . . . take something that wasn't mine, or make a big deal out of this, or anything like that. I didn't want him to see me differently. "She was beautiful." It felt like my chest tightened and, conversely, a weight was lifted off me. "I wanted to ask for her number, but what was I gonna do? Date her for a couple weeks and go home?" I tried to be casual about it.

Another long silence. "I didn't know you were bi. Or pan?" he added hastily. "I didn't know."

I hadn't wanted him to focus on that. But maybe I had. Maybe I wanted it out there, so I could face it.

"Well, it's not like I go around wearing a sign," I joked, but my voice was a little tight, and I realized that I was waiting for him to judge me. Even though he was gay, even though he was in a relationship with another man. I was waiting for him to tell me I couldn't be who I said I was. It was what I was used to.

He laughed. "Well, no. I just feel like I should, I don't know . . . have some way to . . ." He trailed off, and I could almost hear his embarrassment over the phone.

"A way to recognize us?"

He groaned. "That sounds so bad."

"It's *so* bad," I taunted. I felt like laughing out loud. Not because of what he was saying, although that was funny enough, but because I was so incredibly relieved. I'd essentially come out to him, and he was concerned only because he hadn't seen it before. "You're stereotyping people."

"I'm not!" He laughed. "Tell me about your girl. What was her name?"

And that was it. He didn't judge me. He didn't ask me something ridiculous, like how long had I known. He didn't tell me that bisexuality was a myth. He didn't make me uncomfortable. He didn't tell me I was wrong.

That was why I liked Micah. He liked everyone best when they were themselves. Whether that self was messy or damaged or perfect or strange or awesome. I hadn't met anyone who saw things quite like that before, and for a second, I was jealous that Bellamy had snagged him. And then I was just glad that he was in my life.

"Cara." I took a breath. "Micah. Do you seriously not care that I'm bi?"

"Why would I care?" He sounded genuinely confused. "I feel bad I assumed you were straight, though."

I pressed my lips together and tried not to make a sound. Suddenly, unfathomably, I was afraid I was going to cry. I kept staring out the window, kept the phone pressed to my ear so I could hear the soft sounds Micah was making as he moved around the kitchen.

"Ava," he said when I'd been quiet for a while. "Do the guys know? Quinn and Tuck? Bellamy?"

I rocked my head back and forth on the pillow. "I don't . . . I don't know." I honestly didn't. It wasn't as if I'd kept it a secret. I'd slept with girls and guys in college, and I didn't think Tuck could have missed that. But I definitely drifted toward the straighter end of the spectrum, if you could use something so simple as that to judge sexuality. The guys I'd brought home outnumbered the women, and it would have been easy for me to . . . hide. And maybe I had a little. Pretended, to make things easier. And I didn't talk about it. I'd never wanted to . . . be the person who stood in the spotlight. Bellamy had always been so open about his sexuality and what it meant to him. I hadn't wanted that, and, more importantly, I hadn't wanted to steal any of that from him either. But now that Micah was asking me and I was actually wondering what the answer was, I realized it sounded an awful lot like keeping who I was locked away.

"I'm not trying to keep it from them," I said. "I don't want to hide it."

"Okay. But it's yours to tell, all right? Not mine. Definitely not mine."

I sighed. From downstairs, I could hear the rumble of my father's voice. I had to get going, get on with my day. "Thank you," I said to Micah.

"For what?"

I closed my eyes, blocking out the daylight, then opened them and let it flood back in. "Just . . . for talking to me."

"Any of us would do that, Ava. They love you, you know."

"I know." And I did. That was the thing, always the sweetest and the hardest thing, at the same time. I was loved. Bellamy loved me and Quinn loved me, and Tuck loved me too. He just didn't love me in the way I loved him. "I have to get going."

"Okay. Call me any time you want, okay?"

"Yeah."

"And Ava? Next time, get the girl's number, all right? Don't . . . don't worry about what might go wrong. It's worth it."

"You saying that from experience?" I wanted it to sound like I was teasing again, but it didn't quite. I wasn't sure when this conversation had gotten so serious.

"Yeah, I am. I'll talk to you later."

We hung up, and I lay there for a little longer, the phone on my chest. I wanted to absorb the whole conversation—it had been short, but it had felt important. Like it had been something I'd needed and hadn't known. But while I was glancing at the clock and wondering how much time I could actually kill staring into the green leaves of the oak tree, my phone buzzed with a message from my cousin. He was at my aunt's place already. We agreed on a time to meet, a little later in the afternoon, and I levered myself up and made myself go take a shower. No more thinking about Micah or the band or Tuck or Cara. Not right now.

chapter two

I left the house early. I told my parents I was meeting Zevi, but really I just wanted to escape before we could have any conversation deeper than the minor ones we'd had this morning. I didn't have a destination in mind, other than eventually arriving at the restaurant Zevi and I had agreed on. I took the same back roads I'd come in on, let them lead me through tiny neighborhoods I'd mostly forgotten about. They came out in the weirdest places. A narrow stretch of worn street, meandering through dense trees, suddenly dumped me into the middle of a town, with a busy rotary and impatient drivers. I followed it and it took me past warehouses, through tight clusters of businesses—cafés and hairdressers and art studios side by side. Then I was in the woods again, until the road opened back up and I was in another center of business. I'd forgotten how patched together everything was here, like no planning had ever happened. I'd never noticed how cramped everything felt until after I'd left.

I found myself driving by a club I'd gone to every weekend, when I'd still been living here. It was a shithole—lighting that was dim because the fixtures were old and dirty, rough concrete walls, a sticky floor. Everything you'd expect from a tiny concert venue, except somehow grungier, dirtier, more closed in. I'd loved it, though. They'd always had good bands, good drinks. It had been one of my few oases, and one of the only places I'd missed after I'd moved. I parked on the street and sat in the car and stared at it.

It looked exactly the same. Flyers, hung with strips of masking tape, were stuck to the windows. There was graffiti along the bottom bricks, old swirls of blue and green, and cigarette butts littered the ground outside. It was closed now, so early in the day, but I got out and walked to the door, pulled on the handle out of habit. It was locked, of course, but the smooth metal bar felt good under my hand.

Escaping Indigo had never played here. All our tiny, cramped venue shows, played to a handful of people, had happened on the other side of the country. We'd toured the West Coast until people were actually coming to see us, until they'd started buying the handmade CDs we'd brought with us. By the time we got to touring the rest of the US, we were playing clubs bigger than this one. It made me proud, sure, but it made me a little sad that we'd never stood on the stage here. That would have made me feel, maybe, like I'd really arrived, in the oddest, most backward way ever.

I wandered over to the flyers and read through the bands and dates. There were a few bands I recognized—I liked listening to small bands that were starting out. It felt good, and a lot of the time, the music was fantastic. Most of the people playing here I had never heard of, though. That was okay with me. A show was a show. I tried to find the flyers for who was playing over the next couple of days. Zevi would go with me if I asked. He was always up for a concert. There were a handful of bands playing tonight, in a local showcase. I took a picture of the flyer with my phone before I hopped back in the car. I was tired already, and I didn't know if I'd be able to make it through all of the bands playing, but if Zevi wanted to go, I'd love to at least catch a little bit. Music, especially live music, happening right in front of me, was my safe place. If we went, it would probably go a long way to loosening some of the knots in my mind, reminding me that everything was fine.

When I finally got to the restaurant, only a few minutes past the time we'd agreed to meet, Zevi was already at the bar. He grinned when he saw me, and patted the barstool next to him, like we met up this way all the time.

"Starting early?" I nodded at his drink. I was only joking. The drink was an iced tea. Zevi had been sober for almost seven years.

"Figured I'd wait for you before I got a table."

I slid onto the seat next to him and leaned back so I could look at him. He seemed the same as always—dark hair, olive skin, a lean build that was just on this side of skinny. He stared back at me, taking me in the same way. It was at once surreal and comfortable. It had been a long time since it'd been the two of us together.

"How've you been?" he asked, and it sounded less like a social pleasantry and more like he actually wanted to know.

I shook my head instead of answering. Zevi was a year younger than me, and growing up, there hadn't been anyone I'd been closer to. We'd lived in the same town then, gone to school together, done everything together. He'd been my best friend. The person I trusted more than anyone. He'd been one of the first and only people who I'd told about my dream to become a musician. He was one of the few people who I'd come out to about being bisexual. He'd known me, the real me, better than anyone else, and I'd thought I'd known him too. Then I'd gone to college and Zevi had gone to work, and it was as if we'd fallen apart. Like a chasm had opened between us. I'd been so wrapped up in my own stuff and trying to get out, get away, that I hadn't even known he'd been having problems. I'd never seen it. He'd gone to rehab a year after I left. I hadn't come back, at the time. He'd told me not to, and I'd taken his word for what he wanted, but I still felt guilty about it.

We were okay now. We'd patched some kind of relationship back together. We talked often, on the phone or through email. But I hadn't seen him outside of a family gathering in years, and things between us weren't like they'd been before.

It still felt good to sit next to him. He grounded me like the music did. He reminded me of who *I* was.

Zevi tipped his head away and stared down at the bar. I thought he was smiling a little, but I couldn't quite see. His fingers played in the condensation on his glass. "You look good, Ava."

I laughed. "You're the first person who hasn't told me how tired I look."

He nodded and glanced back up at me. "Yeah, but it's like the good type of tired, you know? Like you worked for it."

I shrugged. Maybe that was true. Or maybe I was just worn down.

"How's the band?" he asked, like someone would ask about family, and I smiled, because they were my family, as much as Zevi and my parents were, and Zevi knew that.

"Good." I waved at the bartender and pointed at Zevi's tea, signaling for the same. "Bellamy met someone new, like I told you last email. I like him a lot." During our infrequent phone calls and frequent emails, Escaping Indigo and the people in it made up a lot of our conversation. He knew about Bellamy, and Tuck and Quinn, or as much as I felt I could tell without delving too deeply into personal things. Neither of us liked gossip, and I wouldn't have done that to my band anyway. But when I worried about Bellamy or was heart sore over Tuck, or when I simply wanted to talk about the things going on with the people in my life, Zevi was there to listen.

"Good for him." He leaned a little closer over the bar. "And Tuck? You still pining over him?"

His words were light, and I tried to laugh. "He's still with his girlfriend. They're totally in love."

"Ahh, Ava. I'm sorry."

I waved my hand between us. "It's fine. It's good." I kept reminding myself of that. Maybe if I repeated it out loud to enough people, I'd actually start to believe it, in the tight, bitter place inside me, and not with only my logical brain.

He narrowed his eyes at me, and I figured he wanted to say more, or maybe ask me something, but he didn't. He shook his head, and we went back to talking about everyday stuff, how our families were doing, and what the plan was for the rest of the week. Neither of us knew how long it would take to clean out our grandmother's house, but we had a date in about two weeks' time for when she was supposed to move in to the new place, so we at least had a rough time frame. I'd booked my return ticket, but I could always change it if I needed to stay a little longer.

While we ate, I told Zevi about the concert happening tonight, and he was eager to go. It had been a long time since we'd gone out together, and I think we were both excited about it, and maybe a little nervous too. It was different hanging out with someone when you hadn't been together for a while. Trying to fall back into old patterns and habits that weren't quite there anymore, didn't quite fit, or fit so well it was surprising and unsettling. You never knew if it was still going to work, or if you were both going to end the evening feeling awkward and weird. But dinner together was good, and I wanted to spend more time with him.

We drove to the club separately but found each other outside, and once we'd paid the cover and were inside, we both, without any conversation, wandered up front and claimed spots near the stage. Zevi turned to me, ready to ask if I wanted a drink. He had always bought first round, I had always bought second. That was all we'd have—those were the days before Zevi had become an alcoholic. He opened his mouth, caught himself in that old habit between us, and a huge grin broke out on my face.

He smiled back at me, just as wide. "I missed this. It doesn't feel any different."

I shook my head, relieved to know that this could still work between us. "It's good, right?"

"Yeah. What do you want to drink?"

I asked him for a soda, and when he wandered off toward the bar, I turned back to the stage. The opening band was climbing the stairs to take their places. They were young, but they had a confidence about them I liked. They already had everything all tuned and setup and ready to go, so there was none of the awkward faffing around that a lot of bands who aren't quite used to being on stage do. They launched into their first song, and I thought they had a good sound, a nice hook with an interesting rock melody behind it.

I found myself swaying to the music, finally relaxing for the first time in a couple of days. For the first time since I'd left my band, when we'd finished our tour and we'd gone our separate ways. Music was where I belonged. This right here, this space by the stage, the heavy thump of the drums and bass, the slide of fingers over guitar strings, the heat and the dark, was the only place I wanted to be, the only time when I truly felt like myself, whether I was the one playing or listening. As long as I was in the middle of the sound and the pulse, I was home.

Zevi came to stand beside me again, handing me a soda in a sweating plastic cup. He didn't try to talk to me or say anything about the band. He knew that when music was happening, my focus wasn't on who was standing beside me. Zevi had always been good at understanding what people needed, and he'd always been good at reading me. Knowing me.

We watched the band perform a few more songs, and Zevi and I sometimes turned and smiled at each other when they played something really good. They had talent. Between songs, I watched the band grin at each other, and I peeked at the people beside me, wondering if they were enjoying the show as much as I was. They seemed to be, and I was happy for the band.

The second time I did it, my attention caught on short tawny hair, pink and blue under the lights. I craned my neck, trying to get a better view, telling myself I was imagining things because I wanted to see that very hair so much. I stood on tiptoes, and Zevi shifted beside me. I glanced over at him and he lifted an eyebrow, but I shook my head. I didn't want to say anything and have it not be true, have him think I was imagining things.

I looked again, and the hair, and then the rest of the girl, drifted for a second, with the slight movement of the crowd, into sight. Cara. It was definitely her. I'd only met her the once, but I recognized her, probably because I'd done so much thinking about her since early this morning.

I turned back to the band before she could see me, or catch me staring. I tried to focus on the music again—it was still good, still as listenable, and I was still as interested, but I couldn't keep my focus anymore. The idea that Cara was there, standing somewhere behind me and off to one side, was completely distracting. I didn't know what to do. Yeah, we'd shared a flight, and some good conversation, and I'd enjoyed meeting her. I'd wished to see her again. But I hadn't thought it would actually happen, and when it came right down to it, we were strangers. It would be weird if I went over to say hello. Wouldn't it?

The band wrapped up their last song, and as they were leaving the stage, I saw Cara move closer. One of the guitar players leaned over the side of the stage, and she reached up to hug him. Those same graceful movements, that elegance in the way she held herself. I couldn't take my eyes off her, even though she was currently hugging someone who most definitely wasn't me. Even though why she was here and what she was doing were really none of my business.

Zevi stepped closer to me, so our shoulders bumped. I looked over, up into his face, and he raised an eyebrow. "You okay?"

I nodded. I opened my mouth to tell him I was fine, but then I found myself grinning at how ridiculous I was being, how ridiculous, really, this whole thing was. "I met a girl on the plane."

The eyebrow inched up even higher, and the other joined it.

I pointed, my hand at my waist so I wasn't completely obvious, to where Cara was talking to the guitar player while he coiled cords and got ready to move his effects box. "That's her. Right there."

Zevi laughed, but when I smiled back, half-embarrassed and wholly unsure of why I was telling him, or what, if anything, I should do, his laughs slowed and stopped. "Seriously?"

I nodded.

"Okay." He glanced back to Cara, then to me. "So, when you say you met her . . .?"

I chewed on my bottom lip. Zevi knew about me, and he'd never cared before, but there was always something a little bit nerve-racking for me about bringing it up. "We sat together?" I said, and it came out like a question, like I wasn't sure of this basic fact. "She let me stretch out and sleep. And then we talked."

He widened his eyes, and his eyebrows went even higher, which, if asked, I would have said was impossible. "And?"

I barked out a laugh, but it sounded almost more like a hiccup. "And what?"

He sighed. "And she's gorgeous? And you obviously can't stop staring at her?"

I shoved my bangs back from my face and sighed. On stage, the next band was setting up as quickly as they could, uncovering a drum set, bringing out guitars. It was a good club, run well, the kind of place where you wanted to see a show, and I wanted to lose myself in that, forget about anything else. But despite not even looking at her, I was so aware of Cara standing there. I didn't know what it was about her, exactly, that made me feel like she was a magnet and I was a helpless bit of iron filing, but I did. It was as if she pulled at me, even when she didn't know she was doing it.

I wanted to turn and glance behind me again, see if she was still there, but I was too nervous. I made myself concentrate on Zevi, his familiar face, those soft brown eyes that looked more grown-up now than I remembered. That looked like they'd seen something of life while I'd been gone. And right now they were giving me this look that was somewhere between frustration and pity. I wanted to do something to make it stop.

"What do you want me to do?" I kept my voice low, as if Cara might overhear me, even though there was no way she could with the rumbling shush of the crowd talking, the overhead music playing while the next band finished setting up. In a minute, it wouldn't matter what Zevi thought I should do, because the lights would go down and the music would be too loud to talk over, and that would be that.

Zevi opened his mouth to say something, but before he did, I gave in to the tug and glanced over my shoulder. This time, Cara wasn't gazing up at the stage, wasn't carrying on a conversation with someone else. She was staring right at me.

I felt my mouth drop open, so I was standing there staring back like an idiot. But I was turning toward her too, my body twisting on its own. She raised her hand, slow, to shoulder level, and waved it once. It took a second, but then she was smiling, the shy grin spreading in tiny increments.

Zevi leaned over so his mouth was near my ear. "At least get her number, for Christ's sake." He gave me a very gentle push, his hand flat between my shoulder blades.

I laughed, surprised and nervous, and stumbled forward. I had to weave through people to get to the other side of the stage. I felt like I was on autopilot. Like I hadn't really made the decision to walk over to her, but I was doing it anyway. I couldn't decide whether I was happy about it or not. Cara had started to move toward me too, and we met in the middle, crowded by people, the next band doing a quick, loud sound check that made it hard to say anything.

"What are you doing here?" I asked stupidly.

Her smile went even brighter, lighting up her whole face. She gestured at the stage, to the side, where the first band had disappeared into the back. "That was my brother. His band."

Not exactly what I'd expected. A rush of relief washed over me, and I berated myself for it. Simply because he was her brother and not her date did not make her available. "You didn't tell me your brother was a musician."

She shrugged. "I didn't want to be one of those people who turns every bit of conversation back to them. I wanted to know about you." It was nice to hear, but I immediately started wondering how often

I did that, related things back to me and claimed them. Too often, probably. I felt myself flushing, for more than one reason.

"They were really good," I said, but just then the next band started up, and their music covered my words.

I glanced at the stage, then back to Cara. I wanted to talk to her, but it was unbearably rude to leave or talk over a band, unless they were rude themselves. Not everybody understood that. But it seemed she did. She smiled at me and turned to the stage, and I was even more relieved. I tilted my head the other way and looked for Zevi. He was standing where I'd left him, and I felt bad for ditching him. I'd come here with him. Talk about rude. I tried to catch his eye, and when I did, I waved for him to come over. He smiled and shook his head, though.

Cara and I watched the set together. She swayed to the music, and sometimes her hip bumped gently into mine, but I didn't move away or give her any more room. I'd have been an idiot to do that, even if I was being obvious. I wanted her to touch me, wanted her to put her hand to my shoulder like she had on the plane, wanted her to dance her way into me, even if it was by accident. I wanted to feel her, wanted to feel, maybe, a touch that wanted me. As simple as that.

The second band was good, although not, I thought, as good as Cara's brother's band. Those kids were going to go far, if they could get through all the nonmusical bits that came with being a band. I immediately felt old for thinking that, and for thinking of them as kids. I remembered one of the first times I'd been on stage with Tuck and Bellamy. We hadn't even had a name then. But I hadn't felt like a kid, and I didn't think they had either.

I tried to pay more attention, but by the time the current band got off the stage, I was yawning and couldn't stop myself. The long day and night before were catching up with me. As much as I wanted to listen to the last band, and be with Zevi, and talk with Cara, I was going to embarrass myself if I stayed any longer. This was my chance, while no one was on the stage, to go.

I turned to Cara and found her staring at me, laughter playing along her lips, before her own yawn had her covering her mouth.

"Been a long day, huh?" I felt some of that easiness that had been between us on the plane.

"Like you can talk." We stood there, on the verge of exhaustion, grinning at each other like fools, until Zevi came up behind me and touched his hand to my arm.

For a second, an expression of complete confusion crossed Cara's face, and then she smoothed it out, her face going blank instead. She nodded at Zevi. I could tell without even looking at him that he was probably grinning from ear to ear, but Cara didn't smile back. She seemed . . . almost jealous, except jealousy wasn't an expression people really wore. But the careful way she was keeping her face blank, the way she had her arms crossed over her chest, made me think that was it. I wanted to laugh, because there was no reason at all to be jealous of Zevi, but at the same time, something warm and sweet swelled inside me. Maybe she really was into me after all, or at least interested.

"This is my cousin," I said, a little louder than we'd been talking before, so she couldn't mishear the words. "Zevi. Zevi, this is Cara."

And there was what seemed to be a tiny flash of relief. There and gone so quickly I couldn't be sure, but it *looked* like that, and I wanted it to be enough that I was going to go with it. She unfolded her arms and stuck out her hand. "Hi."

Zevi reached around me to shake with her, and when they pulled apart, he turned to me. "I probably need to get going. Early day tomorrow."

I nodded. "I should go too." I wasn't sure if I was telling Zevi or Cara or myself.

Zevi poked me in the side, not so subtly, and leaned in to whisper in my ear. "Get her number. Or I'll do it for you."

I was probably going beet red. I looked up, and I knew Zevi hadn't whispered quite quietly enough. Cara was smiling again, and her own cheeks were a darker pink than normal. I cleared my throat.

"Umm." You'd think I'd be better at this, have a little more confidence in myself or something. Rock star, toured the world, stood on stages and listened to people scream for my band, but when it came down to it, I was afraid to ask a pretty girl for her number. I guessed rejection never really got easier, no matter what else happened in your life or who you were. "I'm only here for a little while," I started, because I figured that was only fair, to remind her. "But I'd like . . . I'd love to call you and maybe . . . get coffee sometime?" I wanted to kick myself for sounding so formal, and phrasing it as a question. Behind me, Zevi tensed, and I figured he either wanted to do the same, or he was trying not to burst out laughing.

Cara was staring at me, and I opened my mouth to start babbling some more, to forestall her saying no. I didn't want to hear it—it was perfectly all right for her to say it, but for some reason, I knew that it would crush me. It had been such a long time since there had been anyone I'd want to call. I slept with a lot of people. There were always fans on the road willing to throw themselves at a band. I wasn't perfect, and sometimes I got lonely. Maybe if I'd done it often enough, or maybe if I'd been kinder, paid more attention, talked more, there might have been someone among all those shifting faces who I wanted to see again, whose number I wanted to have in my phone. But as it was, there was no one, had been no one, in what felt like forever. And Cara . . . no, I didn't know her. Had barely met her, really, but I knew already that I liked her. And I wanted her to like me enough to say yes.

She held up a hand as I took a breath, cutting off whatever inane thing had been about to pop out of my mouth. She grabbed her cell out of her back pocket and handed it to me. "Here. Put your number in."

Okay. Well, that gave her the option to let me down gently—take my number, make like she was going to call me, and then conveniently forget. But at least neither of us would be as embarrassed as if she said no right here. I took the phone from her and opened the contacts. For a second, I thought about not putting anything but my name, a way to tell her later, if she bothered to check, that I got it. But that was petty and bitter and childish, and I ended up putting my number in.

She took the phone back and messed with it, and a second later, my own phone buzzed in my bag, against my leg. "There," she said. "Now we have each other's numbers."

I knew my mouth was probably hanging open again, but I was surprised and . . . so absolutely fucking delighted, I couldn't do anything about it. "You . . . you really want . . ." Maybe I was too tired for this. I couldn't form proper sentences. Maybe I'd fallen asleep in the club and I was dreaming.

Zevi grabbed me by the elbow. "Okay, good. Time to go." He gave me a sharp look, and I shut my mouth. He turned to Cara. "It was nice to meet you."

She nodded and turned to me.

"I'll call you," I said, still a little dazed by how lucky I was tonight. I hadn't kissed her, hadn't gotten the promise of a date from her, but I'd run into her again, and she'd been interested enough in me, so that was how I felt. Bellamy would call me fortunate, because he loved words like that. Fortunate and a little bit special.

Her lips moved into that soft smile again. "Yeah. Do."

"Tell your brother I thought his band was really good." Zevi was tugging me toward the door, and I had to look over my shoulder to talk to her as I stepped away. She was already disappearing, the crowd closing in on the tiny space we'd left between us.

"He'll love that, coming from you!" she called. I waved and she waved back, and then I turned and followed Zevi out of the club.

"Sorry," he said when we got out the door. "I know you. Didn't want you to put your foot in your mouth any more."

I shook my head. I almost said I'd been tired and not thinking clearly when I first met Cara, and had probably already made a fool of myself in front of her. I *was* tired all of a sudden—exhausted, like my last reserves had left me in the club, in those few minutes with Cara, and now I was running on fumes. I needed to get back to my parents' house and get some rest.

"I'll see you tomorrow morning?" Zevi asked, walking backward as we each headed to our cars.

I nodded. "I'll meet you there."

He waved and turned around, and I made my way to my car, and then to my parents' house. It was dark when I got there, only the porch light on for me, and I remembered the thoughts I'd had this morning, about sneaking in and out. I used my key and let myself in, and went up to my room without any sneaking at all.

chapter three

I woke up closer to noon than morning the next day, the flight and the whole day before finally catching up with me. When I came downstairs, my mom was standing by the coffee maker. She had mugs and spoons lined out just so, and she handed me one when I came to stand next to her. She gave me a once-over, eyeing the ratty band T-shirt I'd worn to bed, the circles under my eyes, my chipped nail polish. I wanted to drop my head and slink away, tuck my nails into my palms. I hated that she could still do that to me, even after all this time, without saying anything at all. Make me feel lacking, make me want to promise to do better when I actually didn't feel like I needed to change anything about me.

I made myself simply stare back at her. For a second, neither of us said anything, and I wondered, for that moment, what would happen if I outright asked her why she was always so disappointed by who I was, why she always wanted me to be someone I wasn't. Would she even admit it? I doubted it, and I didn't want to find out. She sighed, and I turned to the coffee maker, and nothing happened.

"Are you going to Grandma's today?" she asked while I stirred sugar into my coffee.

I nodded. "You?"

She brushed her hair back from her face, a quick, careful flick of her fingers. The kitchen was so bright, even though it was cloudy outside. The gray of the day seemed to magnify the light, make it feel like it was surrounding us. My mother seemed to be basking in it. I tried to remember what she'd looked like sitting at the table in the house where I'd grown up. In the shade of the trees, the light completely different. I couldn't picture it anymore.

"Later. Dad's picking up some furniture, and then he's going to come back and get me, and we'll bring it to her new place."

I nodded and then . . . I just stood there. I didn't know what else to do, or say, and it didn't seem like my mom did either. I held my coffee cup in front of me with both hands like it would protect me from how awkward this situation was. When had this happened to us? My mom and I had never been super close, but she was still my mom, and I was still her kid. She'd been the person who knew me better than anyone, who knew everything about me. But somewhere between my teenage years and where we were now, it was as if we'd forgotten how to talk to each other. How to be with each other. It made me feel . . . sad and distant in a way I couldn't really explain.

I gestured up toward the stairs. "I'm going to go get ready."

She nodded, and looked almost relieved. I left her twirling her mug around on the table.

By the time I got to my grandmother's house, Zevi's car was already in her driveway. I parked next to him and let myself in the back door without knocking. I wasn't sure if anyone would hear me.

The house was quiet around me, but not quite still. I could feel that it wasn't empty, that people were here, but it seemed like the wood and cloth, the old carpets and thick cotton curtains and soft edges of the place, were soaking up all the sound and light. It had always been like that in this house, no matter how many people were here. Close and cavernous at the same time, suffocating instead of cozy, unless it was winter, and then it was comfortable and snug. With the summer heat pouring in now, though, it felt sticky and smothering.

I moved from the kitchen at the back of the house into the main part, searching for my grandmother or Zevi. I came around a corner and ran almost smack into my gran. I gasped, and she took a step back, the soles of her shoes scuffing on the carpet, the noise just a whisper before the house sucked it in like every other sound.

"You scared the crap out of me." I pressed my hand to my chest, trying to slow my heart. "Jesus."

She shrugged. "Don't sneak around, then."

"I wasn't . . ." I started, but she was already brushing past me. She moved slowly—she had arthritis in her hips and knees, and that was the biggest reason why she couldn't stay in her house anymore—but she was still graceful. Careful, each movement precise. I wasn't sure, honestly, if that was because of the pain or if she'd always moved that way. She walked into the kitchen, and I turned to follow her.

"Hey," I said, but I was mostly talking to her back, the long silver braid hanging down her light-blue shirt. "That's it?"

She glanced at me over her shoulder, then gestured at the juice she was getting out of the refrigerator. "Would you like some?"

I shook my head. I wasn't surprised, exactly. My grandma had always done things her way, a way that wasn't always what everyone else wanted. And if my mother and I had never been close, my grandmother and I had been downright distant. But it stung a little bit.

"I just flew all the way across the country to help you move." I watched as she took a step toward the fridge, then back to the counter. Conservation of movements and energy, like she had everything calculated to what would be the exact, most efficient thing to do.

She didn't even glance back at me. "You mean you just flew all the way across the country to stuff me somewhere out of the way, without asking me first if I even wanted you here."

Ouch. "Well, I'm glad to see your brain and speech aren't failing," I said dryly.

She set her glass on the counter and turned to face me. She gave me the same look, up and down, that my mother had that morning. It felt completely different, though. Less like she was getting ready to criticize me, or size me up, and more like she wanted to *see* me. It was better, but not any more comfortable. I wanted to squirm or duck my head, but I made myself hold still.

She sighed. "You look like you walked all the way across the country instead of flying."

"God. Can everyone stop commenting on how awful I look?" I had peeked in the mirror this morning—fleetingly, sure, but I hadn't thought it was quite that bad. Apparently I couldn't see what everyone else did.

She turned to the cabinet and pulled out a second glass, then went back to the fridge for the juice. "I didn't say you looked terrible. I said you looked tired." She poured the juice, then turned to face me again, handing me the glass. "Do you even want to be here?"

I took a sip of juice so I wouldn't have to answer right away. It was fruit punch, something Zevi and I had always asked for whenever we'd been here to visit.

"I wanted to be here for you," I said, hedging.

She hesitated, then nodded. "Thank you, then. I'm not unhappy you're here, Ava."

I took another sip of my juice, and she sipped at hers. I thought, somewhere in the muffling effect of the house, I could hear Zevi moving something heavy, but neither my grandmother nor I made any move to go help him. We just stood together. It was odd, to be here after so much time and be doing this, which amounted to basically nothing. But it wasn't as awkward as I would have thought, and I liked it more than the banal pleasantries people usually expected you to exchange. It wasn't easier, exactly, but it was real.

"Do you not want to go?" I asked after a minute. It was what I'd been wondering yesterday, but I hadn't expected to be faced with it right off the bat in quite that way.

She shook her head, but it wasn't to say no, I didn't think. "I have to go."

"You don't *have* to," I started, because, really, who wanted to be told they had to leave their house and go live somewhere else, and had no choice in it? But I was a little worried she was going to agree with me, and then what was I going to do? I couldn't exactly tell my parents that Gran wasn't leaving her house and that was that, sorry.

But she was already shaking her head again. "I do." She gestured at her knees. "I can't do this anymore. No one's wrong about that, and I know it. But I don't like it."

"I get that."

"I can't even help you move my stuff." She actually looked pouty, which might have been funny to see on a woman pushing ninety, but it wasn't at all. I'd have felt terrible if people were poking around in my house, my things, telling me what I had to do, where I had to go. If I had to decide what to keep and what to get rid of. It was a nightmare. And I'd never really thought about it before, because moving an elderly relative out of their home seemed so commonplace, somehow. It *was* commonplace. But that didn't make it any less horrifying.

I started to apologize, to say something that might make this better, although what I could possibly come up with that would even come close was beyond me. But my grandma waved a hand in front of her, dismissing me and the situation. "Don't."

"Okay." I had this image in my head that grandmothers were supposed to be cuddly and bake you cookies and, I don't know, knit scarves or something. My dad's mother had been like that—a terrible baker, and I didn't think I'd ever seen her knit, but she'd been old-fashioned and into doing crafts and making puzzles and being . . . grandmotherly. She'd babied me and cooed over all my kindergarten drawings and had been so confused when I'd taken up drumming, but I'd kind of understood because it was so far outside what she knew. She'd been sweet, really, was the best way to describe her. My grandmother here, my mother's mother, wasn't sweet. She was straightforward and blunt and she didn't try to coddle me simply because I was her grandchild. It had made her seem almost rough, cold and hard nearly, but not quite. Just close enough that she didn't feel like a grandmother was *supposed* to. As a kid, that had freaked me out, even when I hadn't really known how to put what was bothering me into words. But as an adult, I almost liked it. It was simpler. And I'd gotten tired a long time ago of things being the way everyone else thought they were supposed to be.

"I can show you everything we do. I can bring stuff downstairs for you to go through." She couldn't go up and down the stairs easily anymore—hadn't been able to for a while.

She shook her head. "No, I trust you two. I've got my own stuff to sort through. Come get me when you get bored, though. There's something I want your help with."

I nodded, and that was that. She went back to her juice, and I turned and headed up to the second floor to find Zevi. My grandmother and I hadn't said hello, hadn't hugged or exchanged any niceties. But I wasn't sure I was upset about it, wasn't sure it stung as much as it first had when I'd walked in. It was, at the very least, real. Honest.

Zevi was sitting in one of the bedrooms upstairs, surrounded by boxes filled with pictures and papers and what appeared to be a whole lot of junk. He looked up when I stepped into the room, and watched while I picked my way through, shoving a couple of things aside so I could sit down, lean my back against the bed.

"You see Gran?" he asked.

I nodded and picked up a handful of pictures. "She's pissed."

He shrugged, but the movement was tight and uncomfortable, and he kept his eyes on the papers he was sorting. "She can't do it here anymore. It's too much. And she'd gonna fall and get herself killed."

"I know. She knows. I just . . ." I glanced around at the room, filled with lifetimes of things. My grandparents' things, my mom's and my aunt's things. Maybe even stuff that went back further than Gran, maybe stuff from her parents, or older relatives, or friends. How much of this stuff had been completely forgotten? Did she even remember what was up here? Or did she remember it all? Maybe it was almost a relief, to have it all sorted through and gone. Or maybe it was like throwing out pieces of herself. I wanted to ask, but I knew I wouldn't. Even if I hadn't been too nervous to, it would have been cruel.

"I kind of hate this," I said without thinking.

Zevi did look up at me then. "Yeah. Me too."

We worked together for a couple of hours, poking through stuff. Zevi had started by going through every single thing, but after a while, it seemed pretty obvious that we would both be as old as our grandmother if we kept that up. We flipped through piles of papers and boxed them, and stacked them near the door so we could bring them to Gran later, to double-check there wasn't anything important. I somehow ended up on the tiny-items-that-seem-to-have-no-place-or-use detail. There were piles of knickknacks, picture frames, costume jewelry, key chains, chunks of wood that might be decorative, if you were into that. I didn't know what to do with all of it. I didn't want it. Zevi didn't want it. My mom would flip if I tried to bring any of it back to her house. But it was someone's life, or it had been, even if it was only junk now. Maybe it had been loved. Maybe it had decorated someone's windowsill or bookcase. Maybe someone had run their fingers over it every day. Maybe it had reminded someone of something, a memory or a person or something good.

I felt terrible throwing it out, but I didn't know what else to do. I boxed everything up and set it by the same pile Zevi was building, and figured that was pretty much all I *could* do.

Zevi and I stopped for a late lunch, snacking on whatever Gran had in her fridge. After, Zevi went back upstairs, and I wandered to the other end of the house, where Gran had her bedroom.

Gran's bedroom had been the best room in the house, the one that was awesome, when I was a kid. She had one of those huge canopy beds, the kind that looked slightly intimidating instead of comfy, especially to a little kid. But it wasn't what dominated the room. Neither was her dark wood furniture, glossy and sleek even while it was clunky. No, the things that had always drawn my eye were the books. Giant bookshelves ringed the room, and continued right out the door, down a tiny hallway and into the connecting study, which was really more of a library. Books and books and more books. The shelves held tons, but she had them stacked sometimes three or four deep, books carefully piled behind books, on top of books, books stacked on the floor in graceful tiers. Books piled on top of the bookcases themselves, books on her nightstand and on the desk in the study. Covers in all colors, with more fonts than I'd ever imagined. Hardcover and paperback, and all different sizes. When I was little, I'd tried to count them, over and over. It had been the most surefire way to get me to stay relatively still for a little while, quell some of that energy that I could never seem to burn off. Put me in the room with the books.

It still looked the same, although I could see that Gran had gotten someone to take down the books from all the higher shelves, and she'd been sorting through them, the same way Zevi and I were sorting upstairs.

She was sitting on a chair in the middle of it all now, books in her arms. She held them carefully and gently, as if they were living things, her fingers tucked around their edges, her palm flat against the spines. It was the same way I held my snare drum, when I had to move it, or my favorite crash cymbal. The way you held something when you absolutely didn't want anything to happen to it.

I rapped my knuckles against the doorframe, and she jerked her head up, startled. She recovered quickly, though, giving her head a tiny shake and setting the books in her lap. She flicked her fingers at me, gesturing me in, and I stepped around the piles of books on the floor. When I got closer, I could see that she'd labeled them with sticky notes, dividing them into categories that weren't quite like any

I'd seen in a library. *Creature novels* was the closest pile. It sat next to a stack labeled *Pirates and buccaneers*. Off to my side, there was *Space opera* and *Fae/fey/fairies*. I couldn't see the rest of the sticky notes, but I wanted to wander around the room and just read them, see how she'd labeled everything else. I had thought my grandmother would be more logical, with a genre system. But maybe this was more logical than the way libraries and bookstores did it, in a way.

I glanced up at my gran. "What are you going to do with them all?"

She shrugged, but it was a lot like the shrug Zevi had given me, when I'd been telling him about how unhappy this was making Gran. A casual thing that didn't mean anything casual at all.

"I can't take them with me. Not all of them." She peered around at the piles, and the books still on their shelves, like I was doing. Then she looked back at me. There was another chair in the corner of the room, and she gestured at it. "Come sit."

I did, careful when I moved the chair so I wouldn't bump it into any of the stacks. When I was seated and facing her, she sighed. Her hands were folded protectively over the books she held in her lap, and she glanced down at them before she brought her gaze back up to me. "These are my favorite things."

I nodded. That was pretty clear. I'd always known that, somewhere in the back of my mind—you didn't sleep surrounded by that many books if you weren't really into them. But it seemed different now, not so much things she liked a lot, but things she loved.

She shook her head. "No, you don't understand. These . . ." She skimmed her thumb over the cover of one of the books. "These are my life."

I shook my head back at her. "I *do* get it, actually. That"—I pointed at the way her hands cradled the books—"is how I hold my drums. You look at those books like Tuck looks at his guitar." It was the first time I'd thought of Tuck since the morning before, and it surprised me. Tuck was usually the first and last thing on my mind, every day. But I'd been . . . distracted.

I didn't even know if Gran knew who Tuck was. I wasn't sure if she knew the name of my band, when it came right down to it. It wasn't something we talked about. It wasn't something anyone but me and Zevi talked about. It was like the family secret—my parents were proud of me. I thought they were, at least. But we didn't talk about my music any more than we had to, and it didn't get mentioned around Gran by extension.

She tilted her head, like she wanted to study me. "All right. You do know, then."

I started to say that, actually, maybe she was the one who didn't know, because my drums were a part of me. They were the basis for everything I did, how I made my living, how I'd found my friends. How I expressed myself and left my mark. Music was my entire world. And I didn't care how many books she'd collected, it couldn't be quite the same. But her fingers were rubbing over the cover again—a shiny modern one. It seemed like she had stuff from her childhood all the way to the present—and I clamped my mouth shut. Maybe it wasn't the same, but these were obviously important. Maybe they were a part of her in a different way.

"What will you do with them?" I asked again, a little bit more gently this time.

She took a deep breath, and seemed to straighten. "I want to sort them all. Pick out my favorites to go with me. As many as I can take. See if anyone wants any of them—you or Zevi. The girls won't, I don't think," she said, referring to my mother and my aunt. "And then . . . some of them are valuable. You can sell them, if you like. Everything else can go to a library. I've already called them."

I glanced around at us. "I don't think we need to sort them for that. Unless you can't remember which are your favorites." It would take us forever. I'd be sorting these things long after she left for the assisted-living place.

She shook her head, slowly. "It'll help the library." She stared up at me, right at me. Her eyes were crystal clear. It wasn't as if she'd gotten old and lost her mind. It was only her body that was failing her, and it wasn't her fault. "Humor me. I want to be with them for a little longer. I want someone to love them before they go."

I couldn't fix her achy knees, and I couldn't *really* tell her, as anything more than a comfort, that she didn't have to go to assisted living. I couldn't make this better for her in any way. Except, I could sort her books for her. I could go through them with her, and by myself if it took longer, and she'd at least know they were being cared for.

It felt silly, even as I thought it, but I knew that if it were me, I'd want someone to do the same. Decide what to do with my drum sets and CDs and the tour stuff I'd collected, with some care. To take the time and remember that these things had been the biggest part of my life.

I let my breath out in a whoosh. "Okay. No problem. Tell me where to start."

chapter four

By the time Zevi came to find me later, the sun was sinking in the sky, and I hadn't even noticed when my dad had come to pick up some of the larger pieces of furniture. I'd spent the afternoon surrounded by the books. I'd thought to maybe do it quickly, but even if I'd wanted to, or if Gran had, I'd gotten distracted by them. Lost in their titles and the beautiful covers. I found myself reading blurbs and first pages, holding them up so my gran could explain them to me, tell me about whatever I wanted to know. She hadn't had room for books she didn't like, so she knew all these backwards and forwards, and sometimes when I held one up for her—most of the time—she smiled like I was reintroducing her to an old friend. She encouraged me to get a box and take anything I thought I might want. I figured I could always ship them. Media Mail was cheap enough, and when was I going to get a chance to get my hands on so many books again? After a while, I even got up and grabbed a pen and paper and started writing down notes about the things my gran said, and tucking the notes into the covers, so I could remember.

I'd never had an afternoon like that, had never had any time like that, with my grandmother. It wasn't like I knew her any better. It was, instead, conversely, like I was realizing more and more how little I knew her at all. But it didn't hurt as much as I might have expected. I was glad to be able to see her as a person, and not just this figure in my life. As someone who had had a life of her own, and still did.

When Zevi was done for the day and came downstairs to get me, he had to clap his hands from the doorway to get my attention. When I looked up, Gran had left her seat, and aside from Zevi, I was alone in the room with the books. I shook my head, trying to clear it.

My eyes were gritty and my hands were dusty. Zevi smiled at me, wry but not quite exasperated, and I wondered how many times he'd called my name.

"What are you doing?"

I gestured at the books. "This."

He stared for a second, but he didn't ask me anything else, didn't wonder about why I was doing this and not something more important, and I remembered all over again why I loved him. Then I wondered why it *was* me doing it and not Zevi. If anything, I'd always thought Zevi and Gran were closer than Gran and I were. But I was selfishly glad it was me. Now that I'd started, I wanted to do it.

I sighed and brushed a hand through my hair, worked a couple of tangles out with my fingers. When I focused again, on Zevi and everything around me, it was like the world had taken a minute to settle back into place. It was almost like I'd been keeping it at bay while I was here in this bedroom. Forgotten it for a little while, tuned out and turned all my energy to what I was doing. And now it was back.

I pulled my phone out of my pocket and checked the time. I saw I had two new messages too. A quick check told me one was Tuck, and one was Cara. Tuck's was long, but Cara's was only a hello and an *It was good to see you*. Short, but it made me go all warm inside. I hadn't known whether to expect anything from her. I'd been too nervous to send my own text. I'd planned to . . . work up to it. Figure out the perfect thing to say, even if it was as simple as her message. But now she'd made it easy for me.

I couldn't spend too much time on either message right then, though. I looked back up at Zevi. "You heading out?"

He nodded. "Dinner with my mom. You want to come?"

I did and I didn't. I hadn't seen my aunt yet, and I probably should. But I wasn't really feeling up to family discussions. I wanted to go somewhere, somewhere I could sit and stare at the text from Cara. Or maybe run for a while. I'd been sitting too long.

And the message from Tuck was still there too. I hadn't called him back yesterday. I needed to talk to him.

I shook my head. "What's Gran doing?"

He huffed out a laugh. "I asked her if she wanted to go too. She told me she needed some quiet time to herself, and to go away."

"Oh." That sounded like Gran.

"I'll see you tomorrow?"

I nodded and he left. I spent a few minutes gathering up books, and then I stood and leaned back, hands on my hips. My spine popped and cracked, stiff from sitting for so long. I hadn't even noticed. I picked up the handful of books I'd been sorting through and stuffed them in my bag. The box Gran had told me to use was almost full, but I wanted to start a couple that had really intrigued me. Might as well bring them with me.

When I straightened, Gran was standing in the doorway, where Zevi had been. She didn't pause like he had, though. She shuffled past me and sank down onto the bed. She flicked out her hand, pointing at one of the stacks of books, and I hesitated, then grabbed the top one and brought it to her. She nodded.

"Thank you. Now you can go."

That was sentiment for you. I wondered, for a split second, if my grandmother loved those books more than she loved me. Then I turned the thought on myself and wondered if I loved my drums more than her. I couldn't decide. I honestly couldn't tell. I knew what I *should* feel, but I didn't know if I did. And maybe that was okay. Fair, in a way, for both of us. Cold, too, to think that way, and I knew most people would pity us both if they knew I was even asking myself those questions. But Gran didn't bullshit, and I didn't want to, either. I knew our relationship was fucked up. Maybe it was better for me to realize that and accept that somewhere, things hadn't gone the way they were supposed to, exactly, rather than try to pretend things were different than the truth.

"See you tomorrow," I said over my shoulder as I turned toward the door.

"Ava." Her voice made me stop and turn around. She was staring at me, taking me in the same way she had when I'd met her in the kitchen. "Enjoy those." She gestured to my heavy bag, and her tone was softer, gentler. A little more personal, in a way.

I nodded once. "Thank you." I found that I meant it. When I walked out of the still too-silent house and tossed my bag full of books in the passenger seat of my rental car, it was like I'd taken a piece of the place with me. Or maybe a piece of my gran. And it was a good piece. A piece I wanted.

I could have gone straight back to my parents', but there weren't any dinner plans, and I didn't feel like going home yet. I took some of the same back roads as yesterday. I didn't know why I suddenly had this desire to drive down roads I'd been down a thousand times before. It was just that I felt like I'd never really seen them. Like they'd been commonplace and now they . . . weren't. They appeared even more different with the setting sun, the light throwing gold shadows on everything, that slight haze in the air that only happened on late-summer evenings, when the sun was still up long past the time it should have been. Maybe it was because I'd seen so many roads over the last few years, traveling from venue to venue. Or maybe it was because it was only now, for whatever reason, hitting me how different this place where I'd grown up was from the place I called home.

Instead of driving through the middle of town again, I took a road that led me, for a while, deeper into the woods, past houses that were tucked so far back it was hard to say what colors they were painted. The street eventually emerged from the trees to run by a lake, and I pulled into the little parking lot in front of the miniscule strip of sand that we'd always called a beach. I parked and got out, did some stretches to work out the stiff places in my muscles from all that sitting. I jogged down to the sand and then back, feeling my heart beat faster.

The beach and the parking lot were deserted now, so I could run around the edge of it in a wide circle and not worry about anyone else being there. In the daytime, it would be full of parents and little kids, getting sunburned while they ate popsicles. Later, when the sun went down, it'd probably be packed with teenagers. We'd come here, when I was in high school, to meet up and smoke and make out. We'd pretended no one knew we were there, that it was our own place. It had always been busy here, but right now, it was empty and quiet, and that was the only thing that made it feel any different than it had before.

I ran a couple more laps, not exerting myself too much, but working off some energy, before I went back to the car and opened the driver's-side door to sit. I leaned back and let the chilly breeze move over me, smelling the rot and greenness of the lake, the way it was fresh and bitter and foreign and familiar, all at the same time. I felt like I was swimming in memories, half-formed sensations and feelings, and I wasn't sure if I wanted to try to escape from them or not.

I dug my phone out of my pocket and called Tuck. I still hadn't read his message, but it wouldn't matter. Tuck and I were always on the same wavelength, always knew what the other was thinking. It was why we were so good together.

It took him a long time to answer, and I remembered the time difference, figuring that, since I was late on my dinner, he might be having his. With Lissa. Maybe they'd gone out. Or maybe they were at home, their home, together, and I was interrupting.

I almost hung up then, flustered with how much that idea bothered me, but Tuck picked up before I could.

"Where have you been?" he asked without bothering to even say hello. "Micah said he talked to you, but you don't answer the phone for me? Baby. Where did we go wrong?"

A laugh burst out of me. I couldn't help it. Tuck was ridiculous, and not really funny at all, but he always made me laugh anyway.

I could hear the smile in his voice when he spoke again, but he was a little more serious this time. "How are you, Ava? Micah said you got there okay and everything."

"Why does everyone wonder that?" I asked. "If my plane fell out of the sky, you would know. You'd have seen it on the news."

He thought about it for a second. "I think it's an excuse," he said finally. "You know. So we can talk to people we miss, without saying something stupid like, 'It's only been a day, but I miss you.'"

My heart thumped hard in my chest. Some days, when it was simply me and Tuck and we were friends like friends should be, I thought maybe I could get over him. Maybe he wouldn't say something or do something that would make me fall for him all over again. Maybe he wouldn't say things that would make my heart act like this. But it never lasted. He was my best friend, and I'd spent most of my adult life standing beside him. He shouldn't be able to surprise me anymore, or make me weak in the knees. But he kept doing it anyway.

"I did tell Micah I missed him," I confessed. "I was lonely, though. Only reason."

He sighed into the phone. There was some noise behind him, like people were talking, or a TV was on, and I heard him move away from it. A door shut behind him, cutting the sound off. "You can always say that to me, you know."

"No, I can't." I chewed on my lip. "Lissa will be jealous. Not supposed to say that to someone else's boyfriend."

"No, she won't. She likes you. And fuck what you're not supposed to do."

"I like her too." And I did. That was the thing. Lissa was . . . genuinely kind. Not that fake, snarky nice that some people pulled on like a cloak, the kind that made you want to slap that niceness out of them so you could see the truth. Lissa was quiet and shy, but thoughtful in a way that was sweet and just fucking awesome. I'd have wanted her around regardless, because she seemed like such a damn good person, without hidden motives. I knew why Tuck loved her, because it was obvious. But she was *with* Tuck. And I was in love with Tuck. And that was the crux of the problem for me.

Tuck was quiet on the other end of the line, waiting. "I wish I wasn't here," I said, instead of saying I missed him. I knew I could tell him that, and he wouldn't think it was odd. But I also knew that if I said the words, I'd put more into them than I wanted to, and I was afraid he would hear it. I was afraid I wouldn't be able to come back from it.

He sighed into the phone, loud enough that I had to pull it away from my ear for a second. "How's your gran?"

"Fine. Sad, maybe. Angry, but that's because she's sad." I took a breath. "I'm going through her books." I wasn't sure why I wanted to tell him that, out of everything, but I did it simply because I knew by now that whatever I felt most like talking to Tuck about was probably the most important thing on my mind. I still wasn't sure exactly how I'd gotten so lucky, to find someone who was so much my perfect match, who was my best friend and made me comfortable and safe, who made me feel loved. But I had him, and even if I didn't think I could tell him I missed him, I could tell him this and know he'd at least try to understand.

"Yeah? Are there a lot?"

I found myself telling him about the stacks of books, the weird way my grandmother was sorting them, the notes I'd started making, and he listened to all of it. By the time I was done, I actually felt drained, but better too. It was good to hear his voice, know he was on the other end of the line, no matter what we said to each other.

We talked about what was going on back home, how he and Lissa were meeting up with Quinn later, how Bellamy was still looking at Micah like he was the best thing that had ever happened to him and didn't seem inclined to stop doing that anytime soon. He asked about Zevi, who he'd met while we were touring, and my parents. It was normal and it grounded me.

The only thing I didn't tell him about was Cara. I wasn't sure why, but I wasn't ready to share her yet. It felt private and personal in a way not many things did. Tuck was someone I shared *everything* with. But, for a little while longer, I wanted to keep Cara separate, here with me and not there with Tuck.

"Hey," he said at the end of the conversation, "Bellamy and I are working on some tracks. Is your old kit still in your parents' basement? I can send the songs to you and maybe you can work out some ideas for them. If you want to." He sounded hopeful and a little bit like he was goading me.

I had no idea if the kit was in the basement, or what state it was in if it was. But I didn't need a drum set to work on really early ideas—at least some of it could be done in my head, with my hands tapping out the patterns on my knees. And the idea of playing sent a zing of electricity through me.

"Yeah, send them. I'll see what I can do."

He agreed to, and we hung up. I found myself smiling after, with the idea of new music and playing drums bouncing around in my head.

It wasn't quite dark out yet. The sun had been sinking lower and lower over the lake, only half of it visible when I'd gotten here. It was just a sliver now, and stars were starting to come out in the dark-blue sky. It was pretty, the type of pretty I forgot to notice all the time. The last red light of the sun on the lake, and the phone call with Tuck, and the whole day before it, had me feeling tired and worn and somewhat nostalgic. I wasn't sure why. I wasn't the kind of person who got mushy over stuff, or was even that sentimental. I just knew it was as if, ever since I'd gotten here, something inside me had been off.

I still had my phone in my hand, and before I could think too much about it, I sent a reply to Cara, asking her something silly about her day. It only took her a second to write back. I hesitated, then pressed down on her number until it dialed. I held the phone to my ear and waited, my heart a tight lump in my throat.

"You know you're never supposed to do that, right?" she asked after we'd said hello. "Respond to a text with a call."

"I don't!" I said quickly, and I heard her laugh on the other end of the line. "I mean, I usually don't." I laughed too, buoyed by how happy she sounded. I wondered if she was always like that, at least part of her happy all the time. "I . . ." I sighed and trailed off.

"What?" She sounded more serious.

"Nothing. Just wanted to talk."

"Okay." It was hesitant, but it didn't seem like she didn't want to talk. "Well, I'm glad you called. Even if it is against the rules."

I laughed. It felt good to talk to her, lighter and easier than talking to Tuck had been. "I solemnly promise not to do it again. What are you up to? Am I interrupting something?"

"No." She sounded like she was walking somewhere outside. I could hear the breeze blowing past the phone, and the slight rush of traffic. "I got out of work a few minutes ago."

"At the dance studio?" I was still fascinated by that. I used my body to make music—drumming was like a full-body sport and mind exercise, all rolled into one. But I didn't make art out of the shapes I took. I didn't bend my body into music. It was different, and thinking about Cara and the way she moved, the long lines she formed, made me want to see her dance. I wanted to know what she looked like under stage lights, wanted to see her body moved by music. I could almost picture it, from her pointed toes to her head held high, but I hadn't watched enough dance to make it real. I'd need to see it for myself.

"Yeah. About to get some dinner." She paused, and I waited. "Do you want to grab something to eat with me? Just casual," she added quickly.

"So, not a date?" I was teasing, but I *did* want to know too. Fishing had its uses. At least it could sometimes get you the truth.

There was another pause, and I stared out over the lake and watched the last tiny piece of the sun sink behind the water.

"It could be a date," she said, soft and slow, like she was afraid I might refuse her if she put it like that. "If you want."

I took a deep breath. I'd been joking, kind of, but now I was tense all over, nervous in that way that was so good but so awful too. "I'd like that."

We settled on a place we both knew, and hung up. It only took me a minute to drive there, but by the time I found a place to park and was standing in front of the tiny restaurant, my hands were shaking. I didn't know what was wrong with me. I didn't get nervous when I hooked up after a show. But I never had much time to think about those before they happened, either. It was only *want* or *don't want*, and that was pretty much it. This was . . . more. More than simply attraction on a physical level. I *liked* Cara.

I wiped my palms on my jeans and pulled the door open. Cara had walked over from her studio, and she was already sitting in one of the worn vinyl booths with the torn upholstery. She saw me right away, and half raised her hand, like she wanted to wave but wasn't sure if she should. I grinned back, probably too wide and too eager, but I couldn't help myself, and some of my nervousness fell away.

It came back almost as soon as I sat down. I didn't know where to put my hands, where to look, whether I should lean forward or back in my seat. Everything I did felt wrong. I couldn't remember the last time I'd felt so out of control of my body. So completely without confidence. I was the confident one. I was the girl who got what she wanted because I worked hard for it. I'd left those parts of my life that made me uncomfortable and insecure and unsure of myself behind when I'd left for the West Coast.

Except now I was back here, so I hadn't really left them as much as I'd thought. And there was a beautiful girl sitting across from me, and I didn't know what to say to her to make her like me as much as I seemed to like her.

She was as gorgeous tonight as she had been the first time I saw her. She was wearing a dark-green hoodie, fleece lined, so it looked extra soft. She had a stretchy tank top on underneath, like something I might wear when I went running. Her mascara had smudged a little around her eyes, and her hair was messy, like she'd washed it and dried it in a hurry without a hairdryer. If she'd been anyone else, I might only have said she was pretty, or cute. But I liked how not-quite perfect she was, how she was real and I could tell that she'd been working. I liked the pink in her cheeks and the way she smiled and how she tapped her fingers against the edge of the table. She wasn't simply cute. She was elegant and strong, and every time I looked at her, I thought again about how beautiful she was.

"You haven't been waiting long, have you?" I asked.

She shook her head. "I ordered our pizza." She'd asked me on the phone what I wanted. I nodded and she nodded back, and I wondered if that was the most conversation we'd be able to come up with. Maybe we weren't any good together unless we were bumping into each other in odd places.

She played with her straw wrapper on the table, twisting the tiny scrap of paper with her fingers. Her knuckles stood out. I wanted to put my hand over hers, not to still her—I was the queen of fidgeting—but to feel some of her energy run into me.

She glanced up at me, not quite through her eyelashes, but almost, so she appeared more shy than coy. "Did you finally get some sleep?"

I nodded, wondering if I still looked tired anyway. I was grimy from working at Gran's all day, and then from my run at the beach, and I wished I'd had time to stop and clean up before I came to meet her.

"Good."

Another nod. My head was going to fall off at this point, and I wasn't sure if we'd ever actually make eye contact. I didn't remember how to do this. The last time I'd been on a date, an actual date that involved conversation more than the prospect of going to bed, I'd been in college, here. It had been before the band and Tuck and Bellamy had started taking up all of my time. And I'd never minded my time going to them. Time for dating later, when I had my own life under control. But now I was wishing I'd at least gotten some practice in, somewhere. Kept my skills in shape, if I'd even had any to begin with.

If it were Tuck or Bellamy or Quinn sitting with me here, this would be different. Easier. I could talk about anything with Tuck, or we could talk about nothing, and it was still comfortable. That's what Tuck always was for me. Comfortable.

"I told my brother you were there last night," Cara said, after the silence had stretched enough that it was starting to get weird. "He was really thrilled." She glanced up again, and there it was, the eye contact. I'd never been much of an eye person, but Cara's were pretty, clear and blue.

"I don't have any sway," I said quickly, holding up a hand. "I don't have an in with record companies or anything."

She shook her head. "I know. He knows. It's just . . . having someone who matters think you're good, you know? I think that's what he wanted to feel. That they were good."

I laughed, but I got that. I remembered when bands I liked had started showing up at our gigs. It had been surreal, and it had meant more than any recording contract I'd ever signed. "He didn't need me to tell him that," I said, though, because I didn't think I was nearly that important.

She smiled, and I realized that she hadn't glanced away since she'd looked up, and neither had I. "Maybe not. But it mattered. Thank you."

When she stared at me like that, it felt like the tiny moment at the start of the show, when there was this drum fill I did that was so small, but there was a pause after it for a few beats. And the whole crowd was waiting for that next beat, when the band came in together and the song really started. That electric anticipation, that feeling of being right on the edge of something amazing. That was what being with Cara was like. I didn't know why. It didn't make sense. But it was good, and I wanted more of it. And in that moment, it didn't seem to matter nearly as much that I couldn't remember how this whole flirting dance went. I let myself forget that I wasn't even sure if I should be here to begin with, taking up her mind. Let myself forget that this was probably selfish. I'd stay and muddle my way through pretty much anything if she was going to look at me like that.

Our pizza arrived, and the sorting out of plates and forks and pizza pieces briefly interrupted us. After that, the conversation wasn't exactly as easy as it would have been if I'd been with Tuck, or even Zevi, but it wasn't quite as stilted as it had been earlier, either. We talked about music and dance, in general ways that we could both relate to. It was odd to see all the ways the two things intersected.

I knew dance used music, but I'd never realized how similar they were. We both told stories. We just did it in slightly different ways—me with my drum set and her with her body.

Cara asked about my family, because I'd told her I was coming back here to see them, and I told her about Gran, but only a little bit. It seemed too depressing for a date, and I was still holding it a little too close, anyway. She didn't need to hear about that. I only wanted to tell her good things, for right now.

When we finally paid and stood up to go, I realized that we'd been sitting here for almost two hours. It was late, late enough that we were both yawning, but neither of us had made a move to leave before now.

My car was parked a few spaces down from the front door, but Cara's was over by her studio, and I offered to walk her. She frowned when I did, pausing outside the door of the restaurant.

"You'll have to walk back alone."

I shrugged. It wasn't exactly a bad neighborhood. And even if it had been, I didn't think I was necessarily in any position to protect Cara more than she could herself. But I wanted to. I wished I could say I was doing it to be chivalrous, but really, I just wanted to be with her for a while longer, even if it was only a few minutes.

She lifted her shoulders, then dropped them. Her hands slipped into the pockets of her hoodie. With the sun down, it was chilly enough to want a jacket, and I wished I were wearing something warmer than my T-shirt.

"Okay." She turned, slowly, toward her car. We ambled along, not in much of a rush, but it still seemed too soon when we stopped outside the glass front of her studio.

"There it is." She lifted her elbow toward the window, the sign painted on the front with the name of the studio and the styles they offered.

We'd talked about the studio—Cara always called it hers, although she'd said she didn't own any of it. She was one of the lead dancers in their performance end of things, though, and she taught classes too.

"Do you have classes tomorrow?" I asked, more to have something else to say than anything.

"Yeah."

"Kids?"

She rocked her head back and forth. "Some. Anyone who wants to come, really. It started as an LGBT+ studio. Dance is a lot more open for that than most professions." She snuck a glance at me, and I wondered if she was actually shy about it. It was the first time either of us had brought up our sexualities, but we *were* on a date. We'd both been pretty clear about that. I didn't think we could really fly the Not Straight flag any higher than that.

Cara shook herself and looked back at the window. "Now we . . . take anyone who needs a safe space to dance, you know? LGBT, people who wouldn't get a chance somewhere else, people who are disabled. Everyone should be able to dance if they want to."

That was a pretty incredible thing to say so simply, and it did something inside my heart, made it jump in a funny way. But I just nodded. If I said anything, I was going to make a fool of myself.

She turned to face me, her expression serious, more serious than I'd seen it all night. "How was it for you? In the band? In the music world? Was it hard?"

"What?" I almost wanted to take a step back. The questions had been so sudden, and no one had ever asked me anything like that before. Not so direct. It had never really . . . been necessary. I didn't have an answer. I didn't even know where to start.

She gave another twitch of her shoulders, and it looked almost uncomfortable. "Being . . . um . . . a lesbian?"

I blinked. I'd known what she was asking. My response had been rhetorical. I hadn't expected her to actually explain. Now I was more flustered than before. And I still didn't know what to say.

"Well," I started, and she stared at me and waited. "I'm not a lesbian, for starters," I said, but gently, because she had phrased it as a question. I'd come across way too many people who thought being bi or pan was a myth, that I was only waiting to pick a side. Cara at least seemed to be open-minded about it. You could never really tell until . . . you were in the middle of it, though. "I'm bi." I wasn't sure I'd ever actually said it out loud like that, so straightforward. With Zevi, I'd hedged around it, finally telling him that sometimes I liked girls too, and that had been enough of an explanation for both of us.

Cara nodded. The movement was tiny, as if she was too focused on me to notice what she herself was doing. I took a deep breath.

"Our lead singer's gay. You probably know that? He doesn't hide it. Had a really messy, public breakup with his previous boyfriend." I stared down at the ground, at the cracked cement of the sidewalk. All the tiny sand grains in it were catching the orange of the streetlights, sparkling and splintering in my vision. "And Tuck . . ." I laughed, but I couldn't tell if it was a happy sound or not. "I think Tuck will love me no matter what I do."

"Oh." Her voice was a breath, a whisper of sound. "You think?"

I didn't know how to tell her that Tuck was one more person who I'd never actually had to say anything to. I *thought* he knew. I didn't think he'd missed those times when I'd taken girls home. But nothing had ever been specifically said about it, either. The fact was, I realized, that I *didn't* know what he knew, or what he thought. Or what he'd think. He did love me, though. I knew that. "We've never really talked about it."

"Why not? Would he . . . would he be uncomfortable with it?" She took a tiny step closer, enough that the soft fuzz of her hoodie brushed my bare arm.

I shook my head. "No." He wouldn't be uncomfortable. He loved Bellamy, hadn't even blinked when Bellamy announced at his first audition that he was gay and had anxiety and we'd have to deal with both of those things if we wanted him. Tuck wasn't the type of person who would judge someone like that, and I wanted to tell Cara that.

But I didn't want to have to tell her that the reason we'd never really talked about it was because it had never seemed that important, in the face of the feelings I had for Tuck himself. All those nameless people I took home (or didn't take home, but took to back corners of the bus, or dressing rooms, or side alleys) didn't mean anything to me except a few minutes of pleasure and stress release. And Tuck meant everything. And that was why I'd never talked about it with him—because I wasn't searching for someone to love. I'd already found him.

I realized that I'd been quiet for way longer than it should take to come up with an answer. "He knows me," I said. "Better than anyone."

It wasn't an answer, not really, but she didn't press it.

"You skirted my original question," she said instead. "But you don't have to answer if you don't want."

I had to think back to what it had been. If I'd had a hard time being bi in the band. Right. "Oh. No. I mean . . . it's probably like dance. Better than most places, but not perfect." That was what I'd seen, at least. It wasn't like I was exactly out. I wasn't a singer, or a guitar player, and we weren't famous enough, either, that paparazzi were following me around trying to determine who I slept with. Like always, it wasn't as if I tried to hide it. But I didn't make a big deal out of it. And it had been . . . fine. "Music's the place I can always be myself," I added, because it felt like the truth. It was the truth. I'd just never quite put it to the test so specifically.

She smiled, slow and sincere. "Good. I'm glad."

"And dance is like that for you?" She was still standing so close, and I wanted to lean that inch further, take a tiny step, so that we touched and stayed pressed together, instead of glancing off each other.

"Yeah." She was still smiling, and she looked almost wistful, or like she was remembering something that had happened a long time ago. "I want to make a space like that for other people, you know?" She sounded shy. I was surprised, honestly, that she'd said it at all. I wouldn't have. I wouldn't have had the courage to admit out loud that I wanted something like that, because it seemed so . . . important. I'd probably have wanted to keep it close, keep all of it close, so it wouldn't hurt as much if it didn't work out. I liked that she wanted to tell me, though, at the same time.

And I did get it. "Yeah." Bellamy had told me once that we had a responsibility. That when we put our music out there, or got up on stage, we were saying things in a hugely public space, and it was our responsibility to make those things count. I knew he thought about that more, since he was our singer, and he wrote the lyrics, the literal words of what we were shouting out to people. But any music could move someone, even if it was only a drumbeat. It could say something. I thought about that, at least in the back of my mind, whenever I wrote my pieces. What I wanted to say to someone who listened to us. I wanted to speak to people, as pretentious as that sounded. I wanted to give people something.

But I wouldn't have said that out loud. Not to Cara. Maybe not even to Tuck. I thought it was brave of her. A simple thing, but a brave one.

"I think that sounds awesome." I felt myself grinning. I liked her. I liked the way she thought. I liked the way she looked at me a little sideways, like she was doing right now, that made me think she was shy and trying to hide it. I liked the way she was so open. It wouldn't be hard to fall for her.

I wasn't sure what that thought did to me. Made me giddy with excitement and possibilities, made me feel lucky, made me terrified because this wasn't supposed to be like that. This was supposed to be flirting and casualness and maybe if I was lucky a bit more, but nothing further than that. Fun for a few days and then I was leaving, because my life wasn't here, would never be here again. And the reason my life was somewhere else was partially because I wanted to go back to Tuck, who I was in love with, even though he wasn't in love with me.

Cara leaned against the building behind us and gazed up at me. "How long are you here for?" she asked, like she'd been staring right into my thoughts.

I shrugged, but the question tightened all the ideas that were forming knots inside me. "I don't know. However long it takes us to clean out my grandmother's house, get everything sorted. Probably two weeks." That's what I'd planned, although I'd also tentatively told my parents and Zevi that I could stay longer if I needed to. Coming here, I'd been crossing my fingers until they'd bruised, hoping that wasn't the case. Now, I wasn't quite as sure.

"And then you go back to making music?"

I nodded. "Yeah. We'll start writing again when I get home. Tuck and Bellamy already are." I wondered if Tuck had sent me the songs he'd told me about, wondered if I'd be able to lose myself in them for a little while tonight. It'd be nice if he had. I could use that.

She nodded too, slower, thoughtful. She was gazing down at our shoes, my black sneakers and her dark-blue flats, my toes almost touching hers. She looked back up at me when she spoke, though.

"Do you want . . . I had a good time tonight. And the other night. Would you want to get together again?"

I knew I should say no, because this had gone from being something that was fun to something I had serious interest in, and I knew the way my heart worked. I'd hurt myself if I kept this up, and maybe Cara would get caught up in that hurt, and I didn't want that to happen. But I couldn't make myself say anything but yes.

"I have to be at my grandmother's tomorrow." I held out my hand on impulse, and she wrapped her fingers around mine, the gesture automatic and comforting. "But I can call you when I'm done? If you're free?" Normally, I'd have told her I'd call her in a couple of days, to make it seem like I wasn't overly eager. But it wasn't like I had time to burn, now. If I wanted to see her before I left, I had to hop on it.

"Okay. Good." She stepped toward me, then back, kind of like she was swaying and kind of like she wasn't sure what she wanted to do, which direction she wanted to go in. Then she stepped in again, even closer than before, right up against me, so I could feel the fuzz of her sweatshirt and the warmth of her skin, and I could smell her shampoo and the lingering scent of basil from the pizza we'd eaten. Then her hand was on my jaw, her fingers resting soft against my neck, and she pressed her mouth to mine. The kiss was soft too, something gentle and sweet. I opened my mouth to it, not necessarily to deepen it, but because I was surprised and happy. I leaned in too, chasing after her, trying to get that tiny bit closer, and I felt her sigh like I'd done exactly what she'd hoped for.

I kissed her more deeply, and she went with me, so I could feel her body lined up all along mine. My hands hovered over her hips, and then I settled them down and tugged gently. I thought kissing would never get old. That surprising warmth, the weird intimacy of being so close to someone. Breathing together. The taste of her on my lips. And when it was Cara, it seemed . . . so much better, even though I was sure I'd probably had more expert kisses. Those kisses didn't seem to matter as much right now.

It wasn't what I'd imagined, probably because when I had imagined it, I'd been remembering all those recent kisses with strangers, how hurried and rough they were. Wonderful and exciting and sexy as fuck in their own ways, and not something I'd want to deny liking, because I did. But kissing Cara wasn't hurried at all. It was slow and hot, and I liked the way I could feel her breath on me, could feel her fingers curling into my shoulder, could hear the tiny sounds she was making. And I wasn't any less desperate than during those hurried kisses, either. Instead, I actually felt more desperate, felt like I couldn't quite get enough, like I wanted to kiss her more and more, until we were both breathless and everything made sense and we were pressed as close together as we could get.

I pulled back at that thought, because it felt like too much, too heavy and too fast, even though as soon as I did, I wanted to kiss her again. We were still standing close together, and I looked at her, looked the tiniest bit up, since she was slightly taller than me, and caught her smiling at me, happy and maybe a little confused and uncertain too. I was definitely confused. That was one of the best kisses I could remember having—not because it was technically perfect, but because I just liked kissing Cara so much, because she was Cara. But the fact that it *was* so good scared me.

I took a step back, so I could feel cool air between us, and she wasn't taking over all of my senses. She seemed almost disappointed. I didn't want that. Not after that kiss. I reached out and ran my thumb over her cheekbone, and watched the color rise up where I touched her skin.

"I should go," I said.

She nodded. She seemed a little dazed. I wanted to pull her back to me, hold her against me, kiss her some more. Maybe ask her if she wanted to come home with me, because my mind was all swimmy with how much color she'd bring to the plain white walls of my parents' house, the sterile bedroom I was staying in.

The thought of it was too good, something I wanted too much, and I backed up again, and gave a half wave. I couldn't ask her. It was too sudden, no matter how much I wanted it, or how much I thought she might want it too. "I'll call." I tried to make myself sound sincere, because I was, but I had to get out of here. My mind couldn't keep up. I needed to *think*.

Cara nodded, and I turned and walked back to my car.

chapter five

I went to bed earlier that night, and the next day I actually saw daylight before noon. My mom wasn't in the kitchen when I came downstairs, and it took me a minute to realize that the silence in the house was because there wasn't anyone home. I glanced around after I got my coffee—I had my priorities straight—and found a note from my dad on the kitchen table. They'd already gone to Gran's to start helping Zevi.

I sat at the table and sipped my coffee and stared at the note. It was almost the most my parents and I had talked since I'd gotten there. I'd missed dinner with them yesterday, hadn't even remembered to call and tell them where I'd be, and they hadn't called either. I wasn't sad about it, exactly. It wasn't that I wanted to have dinner with them, particularly, although I didn't *not* want to, either. I just figured there should be something more there. I thought I should miss them more, when we weren't together, and I wondered if there was something broken inside me because I didn't.

They were still at Gran's house by the time I got there. Mom was in the kitchen, and Dad had started on the upstairs with Zevi. My mom was put out because she'd wanted to tackle my grandmother's room, and Gran had told her not to.

"She said you're handling it," my mom said, turning away from the kitchen utensils she was sorting. She had a spatula in one hand and a muffin tin in the other, but the image wasn't even remotely amusing. Her expression was too stiff for that.

I still wanted to laugh. Just to ease the tension I could feel building. Just to see if she'd laugh with me.

"I am." I tried to sound sure about it. Gran and I hadn't talked about anything but the books, but I figured she'd be taking most of the other stuff in her bedroom with her anyway. It couldn't be that hard, if I did get left doing it.

Mom set the muffin tin down, carefully, so it didn't clatter against the counter. "Did you get the bagel? I left you a bagel for breakfast." She said it quickly, and with a sharp bite to it that was close to exasperation, as if she was sure that I'd have ignored the bagel simply to rebel against her in one more way.

I nodded. It had been in the note. And there had been blueberry preserves to go on it. I wasn't going to pass up something like that.

"Oh. Good." She actually looked surprised. "And coffee? Was there enough in the pot?"

I nodded again. "It was fine. Thank you."

She stared down at the muffin tray, then pushed it gently to the side with the spatula she was still holding. "Your dad and I were thinking maybe we could have dinner tonight?" She said it like a question, and it dawned on me that she was nervous. That maybe she actually imagined I would say no. I was surprised by the question, and then I wasn't. Maybe they had been thinking about the same thing I had, at the breakfast table this morning.

"Yeah, Mom. That'd be nice." I'd told Cara I'd call, and I wanted to. Wanted to tell my mom I already had plans. But I didn't, really—I'd told Cara I didn't know when I'd be done. And I didn't want to be the type of person who picked a possible thing over their own parents.

My mom and I ended our weird little conversation, and I went and found my grandmother in her room. She was sitting in the hallway that connected her bedroom and the office, actually, books spread out all around her feet. She was still pulling them off the shelves, and she barely glanced up when I knocked on the doorjamb.

She pointed at a stack close to me. "I set those aside for you. You can take others, of course. But I thought you might like those."

I steeled myself and picked up the first book. When you were a musician, everyone wanted to give you books about that. It was a nice idea. Something you were obviously interested in. I should have loved reading books where the main characters were rock stars or singers or whatever. And some I did. But mostly I found myself nitpicking them until I'd torn all the enjoyment out of them. I stayed away from them now, if I could, and I wasn't sure how I was going to tell Gran that.

I didn't have to. The book in my hand wasn't about musicians at all. It was sci-fi—something I figured Gran would have me put in her space opera pile if I didn't take it with me. It had a crazy cover, too many colors and faces of characters that appeared half-alien and half-human. But when I flipped it over and read the blurb, I realized it was a lot like some of the books I'd boxed up for myself yesterday. Sweeping and dramatic but still full of space stuff, traveling to different planets, humanity living on the edge of civilization.

I picked up the next book. An obscure fantasy, not something epic. Smaller scale than that. Fairies on the cover, but not the kind with wings and flowers. The kind with sharp teeth and proud expressions.

Gran had been paying attention.

"Did you start any of those books you brought home?" She was still focused on the books in her hands, slowly placing them on one pile or another.

"I did. I didn't get too far yet. They're . . ." I didn't know how to explain it. The one I'd started wasn't like anything I'd ever read before—not because of the genre, but because it was so strange. Strange and dreamy and ethereal and dark, all at the same time, and I was only a few chapters into it, but I thought I loved it. "They're good."

Gran nodded, as if that was all the explanation she needed. "I think you can start boxing up the sci-fi we went through yesterday, to go."

That was a dismissal, but it was fine with me. I walked back into her bedroom, set my own messenger bag on her bed, and then sat on the floor, pulled an empty box over, and started putting books in.

I got totally absorbed in it, the same as I had yesterday. What should have maybe taken a couple of hours took me all day, because after I was done with packing up what we'd gone through the day before, I started on new books that had been pulled off the shelves. And like the day before, I got caught up in reading pieces, in wondering if I wanted to read the books myself, asking my grandmother about them and jotting down notes. I felt like I'd stumbled on a treasure I hadn't known existed. The books had always been there, and I'd been fascinated by them, but mostly in an abstract way. I'd never really considered that they were there to be read, that I could be the one reading them. Maybe I'd been too young before. But now that they were in front of me and I had my hands on them, and I was old enough, I couldn't get enough of them.

And the more I talked to my grandmother about them, the more I thought about what she'd first said, the day before, when she told me the books were her life. I hadn't quite believed her then, but I was starting to. These books were pieces of her. The way she talked about them was the way someone talked about something they loved desperately. The stories she told about the books weren't only about plot, but about the way the books made her feel, the ways they had changed her, where she'd been in her life when she'd first read them, and what they reminded her of. I didn't want to lose any of it—not the books, and not the things she had to say about them.

At the end of the day, I looked up to where Gran had moved, over by her bureau. She hadn't wanted to stop going through the books, but my mom had come in and reminded her that she probably wanted to start packing clothes if she wanted to have anything to wear when she got to the assisted-living place.

"I'm going to take them with me," I announced.

Gran flicked a glance over her shoulder, and then back down, like she wasn't interested. "What?"

"The books. If that's okay with you." I stared at the box I'd packed and carefully marked as sci-fi, with all the subcategories my grandmother thought were important written underneath. There was another sci-fi box next to it, and another. "I want to keep sorting them, and keep having you tell me about them. And then . . . I want to ship them home. I want to take them."

She turned all the way around in her chair then. "Are you sure?" She definitely wasn't uninterested now. She sounded cautious, though. Like she thought I was a little kid who had asked for two slices of cake instead of one. "That's a lot of books. They take up a lot of space."

"I'm not promising I'll keep them all," I said, because honesty was a good thing, most of the time. And there *were* an awful lot of books. I glanced around at them again and wondered if they'd actually all fit in my little house. "If I don't like them, they'll get donated.

But . . ." Another glance at the boxes. No. I couldn't leave them here. I just couldn't. "There's enough room at home." I was already doing mental calculations about how many books could fit in the living room and the spare bedroom. "I think I can manage."

She blinked, and I realized I was actually getting some emotion out of her, something other than exasperation and that straightforward, one direction, no-stopping way she looked at everything. "I've never seen your house," she said.

It wasn't quite what I'd expected. "I can show you?" I made to reach for my phone, because reaching for pictures was an automatic response. But I stopped myself, because I knew I didn't have any pictures of my house. Who took random pictures of their house and saved them on their phone for no reason?

She shook her head. "If you want." She brushed her hand over her forehead, pressing her bangs back. "I'm happy enough to know you have a place you like, Ava. Doubly so if you can fit my books."

That surprised me more than anything. I hadn't figured my happiness really entered into her mind, let alone affected her own happiness.

"I do like it." I loved it, honestly. Not necessarily because it was the best house ever, although I thought it was, even if the counter in the kitchen stuck out a little too far, and there was that spot in the floorboards in the living room that was a little uneven, and the floor in the garage was always mysteriously damp. I loved it because it was a place that was mine, a place to be myself, to be with my friends, that I had bought for myself, with money I made doing something I loved. For me, that was pretty fucking special.

She nodded, and that seemed to be the end of that. I worked for a little while longer, and then got ready to leave, to meet my parents at the restaurant my mom wanted to go to. I asked Gran if she wanted to go, and Zevi too. I was hoping for the support—for what, I wasn't sure, and I didn't think Gran was really into offering tons of support anyway. But Gran told me, again, that she'd had enough of people for one day. Zevi took me up on it, however. He seemed to realize what he'd gotten into when I called to tell my parents he was coming. He tried to duck out, and I wondered if I'd screwed up, inviting him to this thing with them. But my mom said for him to come, and she seemed like she really did want him there. Maybe I wasn't the only one hoping for a buffer.

I was dusty from books and helping my grandmother go through her closet, so I went home to shower and change before we all met at the restaurant. When I got there, Zevi was already at the table, sitting by himself. I slid into the chair kitty-corner to him.

"I feel like we're waiting for our doom," he said, leaning to the side so he could whisper dramatically to me, even though there wasn't anyone there. It made me laugh, and some of the tension I'd been carrying around slipped away from me.

"It's only dinner," I told him, but we both knew I was really telling myself. He nudged my knee with his, and went back to sipping his water.

I didn't know why I was nervous, not really. I'd already had a sit-down meal with my parents. And I loved my parents. My parents loved me. I wasn't one of those kids who'd had a shitty childhood, for one reason or another. I'd been beyond lucky. I'd had everything I'd wanted.

But I felt almost as if, as I'd grown up, we'd stopped remembering who we were. Like we'd lost touch with each other, for all that we lived in the same house.

Dinner started off totally fine, and I was relieved all over again that I'd brought Zevi. My parents asked Zevi about himself and his job. He did something complicated with websites that I'd never quite understood but had always thought was really cool, because it was technical and creative at the same time. I always wanted him to tell me more about it, and he always worried he was going to bore me. My dad seemed to know everything about it, though, and it kept them talking through the appetizers and into the beginning of our main course. I wasn't surprised. My dad was wicked smart. He always knew a little bit about everything, and could talk about almost any subject. When I was little, I used to come to him with all those weird questions kids came up with, and he'd always done his best to give me an actual answer I could understand.

Unfortunately, my parents couldn't really ask about Zevi and not about me. Escaping Indigo and my life across the country was something we'd actually managed to avoid talking about so far.

It should have been impossible, but we'd gotten pretty good at it over the years. It wasn't like they'd never come to one of my shows. They had our albums at their stereo. But we . . . didn't talk about it.

Maybe I could have brushed it off with a one sentence answer, and directed the conversation back to how the pasta sauce at the restaurant hadn't changed at all since the last time I'd been, or to all the things we still had to do at Gran's house, or anything else. But for the first time, having Zevi there made things awkward.

He didn't mean it. It was just that, unlike my parents, Zevi knew almost everything that went on with the band. So when I said we were planning to go back to the studio when I got home, he asked about it. And that started us on a conversation about the last time we'd recorded and how stressful it had been, and the grueling hours we'd put in to get everything done. Studio time was my favorite part of being a musician, because it was like a test of how much you loved what you did. How much work you'd put in to get there, how good your ideas were, how well you could work under pressure and time constraints.

I let myself start to get excited about it. I wanted to get home and start really being able to write, to hear the songs as they were born, and not on my tinny phone speakers, alone in my parents' basement.

And then, while I was talking about how much work it was, my mom made a sound that was almost a snort. A delicate snort, maybe a laugh, really, if I felt like being generous.

I didn't.

"Do you not think it's work?" I asked, stopping in the middle of my sentence and turning so I was facing her.

She went completely white, and I wondered if she even realized she'd made the sound herself. For a second, she looked so uncertain, and I thought she might deny it, or apologize even, and a spike of adrenaline went through me. But then she collected herself, put herself back together and gathered defensiveness around her.

"It's not quite going to work in an office every day, though, is it?" She sounded like she wanted to be halfway between arrogant and gentle. "It's not what other people do."

I should have let it go. It was because I'd called her out like that, in front of my dad and Zevi, and she had to respond to it. It wasn't a big deal. But I had this image of Bellamy in my head, of him slumped over his guitar, his fingers so tired he kept missing notes, this expression on his face like his whole life depended on getting the song right, because in a way it did. I had almost the same image of Tuck and me when we'd first started the band, sitting together in the tiny, dirty van we'd bought together by pooling our money, hoping it would get us to the next gig.

It wasn't like working in an office, no. I was sure there were lots of hard things about office work, or any normal job. But being a musician had its own complications. I couldn't go to work every day and be sure I'd have a job the next. There was no certainty in it. I had to put my whole body into everything I did, and my mind, and my heart. I couldn't leave it behind when I wasn't at work. I had to always be my best, in every way, and so did Bellamy, and Tuck.

"You're right." I knew I sounded bitter, but I couldn't really keep it out of my voice. It just wasn't going to happen. "It's not what other people do. It's not like what anyone else does. It's still my job, though."

"Ava," my dad said softly, and I glanced over at him, unassuming but still fierce in his own way, with his glasses perched on the edge of his nose. "It's only . . . All those times you didn't have any money. When you were living out of that van . . ."

"We were *touring*," I said, vehement.

"You couldn't make rent," my mother said, speaking even louder than me. "You were living on people's couches. The bars you played were paying you in beer!"

"That's how it works!" I glanced over at Zevi, but he was staring pointedly down at his breadstick, which he was shredding to pieces on his plate. "Besides," I added, trying to get myself under control. "It's not like that anymore. I bought a house. I paid for it myself." It was a nice house too. A house I loved.

"Yes," my mom said, and I thought she'd let it go, but then she laughed and said, "Ocean view," and I knew she wasn't congratulating me, or making it something good. She was poking at me.

And yeah, okay, my ocean view was a strip of water and beach I could see through the houses across the street. And yeah, I'd probably paid far more for the house than it was worth, to have that. But I could *see the water from every room*. I had the ocean, right there. I could walk out onto my porch and smell the salt and seaweed in the air. I could feel it on my skin when there was a breeze. Every day, that tiny strip of blue and gold reminded me that I had made it, that I'd brought myself all the way across the country and created a place for myself, and it was a good place. Looking at that water was like looking at victory.

"You have never known what was important to me," I said, my voice so much lower than before. I saw Zevi leaning forward to catch my words, and then jerking back when he heard them.

Neither of my parents responded to that. My mom looked as if I'd hit her, as if my words had physically lashed out and attacked her. My dad didn't seem to know where to look, or who to comfort. He reached out and put his hand over my mom's on the table, and seeing him do that made me feel terrible. Instantly terrible. Any victory I'd had, any point scoring I'd won, was gone, and instead all I felt was guilt at making them feel bad. That wasn't what I'd wanted. I'd only wanted my mom to acknowledge that I'd done something good, come out okay. But that wasn't going to happen, and now they felt bad, and I felt awful.

I stared down at my dinner and picked at it with my fork. There were a few long minutes of strained silence. Then the waiter came around and filled our water glasses, and in the broken tension he left, Zevi started up a new conversation, something completely innocuous. We all went with it, because we didn't want to stick with what we were doing. And that was how we got through dinner. By the time we left, none of us were exactly happy, and I'd been wrung out too many times, but we were still all on speaking terms. I supposed that was a win.

chapter six

I told Zevi I'd meet him back at my house. Then I realized how awful that sounded, to ask him to go there and wait for me, and tried to take it back. But he told me to take all the time I wanted. I gave him the key for the door, and then I walked to my car alone.

It was just that side of sunset when the sun was completely down, but the light was lingering, highlighting all the trees from underneath, turning dull brown tree bark into something gold and glowing and beautiful. I watched my parents pull out of the parking lot and head off down the street. Instead of doing the same, I turned and leaned against my car. I knew I was supposed to get in and lock the door and not sit in the parking lot—safety and all that. It was probably solid, if unfortunate, advice. I was a girl pushing five feet, and drumming had given me some muscle but not much. I wasn't fool enough to think I could take anyone. But I figured that if I could survive alleys between clubs and dimly lit inner-city parking lots, I could handle one in the middle of a sleepy town.

I pulled my phone out and called Tuck.

"Hey," I said when he answered, because I'd had about enough conversations that didn't start with a greeting.

"Hey." He sounded a little bit sleepy, like he'd been lounging in front of the TV or something when I called. "You okay?"

I shrugged, but said, "Yeah," into the phone. I didn't know if I was okay. I didn't know what I was doing here. It had turned out to be so different than I'd expected, somehow different than it ever had been before, like I was seeing it all through a new filter.

"You just don't usually call so often," he explained, and I felt immediately guilty.

"Sorry. Were you doing something? I can call you later—"

"Nope," he said easily. "Not busy at all. Bellamy and Micah and Quinn are here. We're all watching a movie." I knew *all* meant Lissa too. Of course it did. She lived with him now. The two of them were basically inseparable.

"Good." I meant it too. I wanted him to be happy. God, I did. This wasn't the way I'd pictured it, or hoped for it, and it made me feel jealous and bitter and awful. But I still wanted it for him. I'd hate myself if I didn't. I could be seething with jealousy and still happy for him at the same time. That was a surprising thing. I'd never have believed that was possible until I felt it for myself.

The human heart. What a fucking piece of work.

"So what's up?" He was trying to sound more awake. I bet he'd been falling asleep on the couch. He always did that when we watched movies—had to watch them in two or three installments, because he could never keep his eyes open. I caught myself wondering if he'd been sleeping with his head on Lissa's shoulder, or her lap. If she'd run her fingers through his hair, the way I sometimes had when we'd crashed, in those early days, after a grueling show schedule. I wondered if she felt as lucky as I had, every time he picked me to lean on.

Then I shook myself, forcing the images and the wondering and all of it out of my mind as best I could.

"I got the songs you sent," I said, because it was something to talk about. My phone had beeped earlier in the day, and it had been the only thing to drag me out of my obsession with the books. I'd paused to listen to them, and my grandmother had glanced over and seen me nodding my head along to one. She'd turned back to what she was doing, no questions and no reprimands for not working when I should have been. "They sound really good. The second one especially."

"Yeah. The bridge is weird in that one. Skips into a couple measures of three-four before it goes back."

I nodded, and let the parking lot and the gold on the trees and how deceptively beautiful everything was—let the weird not-quite argument with my parents and the distance between me and my family—fade away. I imagined I was there with Tuck, pictured myself in his house. I had to switch, because at first, I pictured him in his old place, the tiny apartment he'd never bothered to move out of, his couch crammed into the miniscule living room. But he'd moved into a house with Lissa, not very far from my own. I had to picture him there now.

When we were done, and I hung up, I didn't know if I felt better or worse. Tuck had passed the phone to Bellamy at one point. I always thought passing the phone was a crazy rude thing to do, normally, but Bellamy had asked to talk to me, and there wasn't ever going to be a time I could imagine when I didn't want to talk to him. And Quinn and Lissa and Micah had shouted hello. And then Tuck had said goodbye and we'd hung up, and I was left standing in the now-pitch-black parking lot, the only light coming from a streetlamp at the other end, with the sounds of their voices in my ears.

I wanted to be back there with them so bad, and I felt crazy for wanting it because it had only been three days. That was all. Three days wasn't enough time to miss anyone. It wasn't enough time to get homesick. But I'd been homesick sitting on the plane, watching the Atlantic Ocean come into view. I'd been homesick from the minute I'd left, and now I had the strongest feeling that all of this was wrong, that I didn't belong here, that I needed to go. And I couldn't.

It was starting to get chilly, and I actually was a little freaked out about standing alone now—not so much because I thought someone was going to attack me, but because the woods were right there, and at night the woods were so black and so thick, and I always imagined they could hold anything at all. I slipped into my car and shut the door between me and them, and then I called Zevi.

"Are you there?" I asked him, forgetting how I'd promised myself I would start phone conversations with real greetings.

"Yup. Said good night to your parents, slipped in the back door. Did you know you have a drum set down here in the basement?"

"I thought I might." I'd meant to check, but I hadn't gotten a chance. One mystery solved. "I'll be there in a few minutes. You sticking around?"

"Definitely." He paused, and I could hear him take in a breath. "But you're sure you don't have other plans?"

Cara had been in the back of my mind the entire day, and all through dinner I'd wished I was with her instead, wished I was back at the worn diner with the excellent pizza, in the booth that, for a couple of hours, had felt like it held the whole world, or at least everything important in it. But now I was tired and probably not super pleasant to be around. She didn't need that.

"Yeah. No."

"Is that a yeah? Or a no?"

I groaned and thumped my head against the steering wheel. "I don't know, Zevi. I told her I'd call. But I'm all . . . worn out from dinner, and I'm not up for anything, and I don't even know if I want to see her again."

"What? Why?" He actually sounded really concerned, and I wondered what impression Cara had made on him in the short time when they'd met. Or what impression I'd made, about needing someone.

"I don't know," I said again, although I really did.

Zevi waited for me to come clean.

I sighed. "She isn't . . . she isn't Tuck."

I could almost hear his frown. "Do you want her to be?"

"No!" I didn't. I totally didn't, not at all. I wanted Cara to be Cara, because she seemed like a girl I could fall in love with. A girl someone would be very lucky to fall in love with. "I mean . . . Zevi. Please don't make me say this out loud."

"You mean you're still all wrapped up around the hope that Tuck will pick you, when almost a decade of evidence to the contrary says it'll never happen." He didn't sound concerned now. His voice sounded flat and angry in a tired way.

"I . . . Yes. How is that fair to her?" I argued. "Besides, I'm leaving. I'm not staying here. I can't get involved with her."

There was another long pause, and I knew he was running over everything I'd said, trying to read between my words. He'd always been so damn good at that. "Are you? Getting involved?"

"Maybe." I didn't have it in me to dissemble with him. Not right now. "Maybe I could. If I let myself."

"Call her," he said sharply.

"Zevi . . ."

"Call her. Tell her we're getting together. Nothing fancy. And invite her to come over too. If she wants to, she will."

"What if I don't want her to?"

"Do you not?"

At least he was kind enough not to tell me what I wanted. At least he had the decency to ask. It made me feel okay, in a strange way, about saying what I actually did want.

"No. I do."

"Then call her. I'll see you when you get here."

He hung up, which I thought was a little rude, but maybe he'd had it with me. I couldn't really blame him. I'd almost had it with myself. I stared at the phone in my hand. There wasn't much debate in me. I wanted to do what Zevi had told me to. So I did.

When I got home, I stepped out of my car in the driveway and stood in the dark, staring up at the lit windows in the living room. My parents were still up—it wasn't that late yet. I thought about going in the front door like I probably should, but my mind skittered away from that thought. It'd be fine. I was sure it would be. I just didn't want to. I went around to the back instead, and through the basement door Zevi had left open for me.

I hadn't been down there since I'd arrived, but I remembered that it had been carpeted and furnished at one point, to be almost like another den. It still was—it was dark and dusty, like no one at all had been down in a while, but with a couple of lamps turned on, the place had a homey, cozy feel. Close, like it was a secret club or something. Zevi must have felt the same thing, because he grinned at me when I came down, and waved, and said hello in a soft voice, as if he wanted to maintain the quiet. I felt like we were sneaking around down here, even though we didn't need to sneak at all, and it seemed like he did too.

The biggest surprise was my drum set. It wasn't set up—neither of my parents would know how to do that—but it was stacked carefully in a corner, all the hardware in a case beside it, the cymbals in another. I couldn't play it now, even if I did set it up, but I went over and ran my fingers over the finish. It was old, the first kit I'd ever had, but it was still a good one. It made me feel funny, in the pit of my stomach, when my hands touched that familiar wood and metal. Like I was happy and uncomfortable at the same time.

I was wondering whether this would be a good time to set it up, so that the next time I came down here I could maybe work on the songs Tuck had sent me, when my phone buzzed in my pocket. I answered it on the second ring.

"Hey, I'm here," Cara said. She sounded a little breathless, like she was nervous. "Do you want me to ring the doorbell?"

I shook my head, despite the fact that she couldn't see me. Across the room, Zevi was smirking, and I wondered what he was seeing on my face.

"No," I said into the phone, giving Zevi a glare. "I'll come get you. We're in the basement."

I thought about how creepy that sounded, but I'd already hung up. Maybe I should call her back and tell her we weren't actually ax murderers. Zevi was almost doubled over laughing, and I contemplated tackling him, but Cara was waiting for me. I didn't want her to get impatient and come to me instead, only to find me and Zevi rolling around on the floor like puppies.

When I'd called Cara, I'd babbled something apologetic about how late it was and how she didn't have to but did she want to meet at my house, and how Zevi would be there so it wasn't like I was calling to ask her for a hookup, but really, she shouldn't feel obligated, even though I really did want to see her. She'd cut me off by laughing, almost as hard as Zevi was now, and said she wanted to.

She was milling around by her car when I got outside, like maybe she was trying to decide whether to make herself go up to the front door anyway. But she saw me right away as I came around the side of the house, and I don't know if it was her smile or that I was exhausted or how honestly glad I was to see her, but I opened my arms. Actually held them out wide. No one really did that, except in dramatic scenes in books. But I really did, held my arms out for her and she stepped into them so I could hold her. She was a little taller than me, and she rested her chin on my shoulder and held me as much as I was holding her. The two of us stood there, pressed close together, in the middle of my parents' driveway. They could look out the front window, where the breakfast table was, and see us, and I didn't care. I didn't care who saw. I didn't care that Zevi was waiting for us down in the basement. I just wanted this moment.

Cara let me hug her for a minute, and then she pushed me back, enough that she could hold me at arm's length and look down at me. "You okay?"

I shrugged and smiled. "Yeah. Fine. Tired." I realized how bad that sounded as soon as the words were out. "I mean, I'm glad you're here. Really glad."

"Yeah?"

I nodded and took her hand. "Yeah. Come on. Come meet my cousin."

She laughed, but let me tug her around the back of the house. "We already met."

"Right. Well." I waved my free hand in front of me. "Meet without having to shout over house sound, then."

She didn't answer, but she squeezed my fingers. I pulled open the back door and led her down the stairs.

I hadn't exactly been worried about Cara and Zevi getting along, but there was always a little bit of nervousness when you were introducing two different people you liked. And the fact was that I didn't really know Cara, not yet. I only knew the surface bits, and I didn't know how those things would go with Zevi. But Zevi was . . . easy. And Cara had been the one to strike up a conversation with me on a plane, so my nervousness about them meeting was small.

Turned out I didn't need to have any, because they hit it right off. Seemed what they were mostly bonding over was me. Zevi took it upon himself to tell Cara all about how I'd been as a teenager, and the last time he'd seen me, and embarrassing things we'd used to get up to in the basement of the house I'd grown up in. That time we'd decided to throw a party and only four people had come. The time Zevi and I had drunk ourselves into a stupor and Zevi had puked down the back of the basement couch we'd used for lounging. And Cara laughed at everything because Zevi was a damn good storyteller.

They were involved in their own little getting-to-know-you world, sitting on opposite ends of the couch and chatting it up, but I didn't feel left out. Actually, I felt better knowing they could get along. I *wanted* them to. And that was a scary thought, because really,

I shouldn't care. I should be thinking of Cara as temporary enough that it wouldn't matter whether she got along with Zevi or not. But I wasn't, and seeing the two of them laughing together did something to me, twisted me up in knots that were tight and uncomfortable and sweet and good.

I wandered to the other side of the room and started pulling the drum set down, laying it out, testing heads. I couldn't play it now, but I wanted to put it together. I wanted to sit behind it. I dragged the pieces closer to Zevi and Cara and sat on the floor in front of them, and they both twisted a little toward me, so we were a triangle and I was included.

"So." Zevi turned to me even further, but not enough that he turned away from Cara. "Dinner with your parents was awkward."

I stared at him, my hands going still on the cymbal stand I'd been piecing back together. Someone had decided it was best to take it all the way apart, instead of only folding it up. "Seriously? We're talking about this now?"

Zevi shrugged like it was no big deal, even though he knew full well it was. Cara raised her hands. "I don't . . . I can . . ."

"See?" I gestured at Cara, but I was still staring at Zevi. "You're making her uncomfortable."

She shook her head, fast. "Oh, no. I know all about weird family stuff. But . . . you don't have to talk about it in front of me if you don't want to."

"Oh, god, no." I looked back down at my hands, focused on the metal against my fingers, the familiar feel of the cool, slick surface on my skin. "It's not you. It's just . . . It's boring."

She leaned against the side of the couch, getting comfortable. "How?"

"Ava's parents want her to be girly," Zevi said, breaking through my tension and stress.

I set the stand upright and waved my hand at him. "That. Well, I mean, that's oversimplifying it a lot, but close enough."

Cara squinted down at me, her gaze slowly moving over me, taking in my painted fingernails, my skinny jeans, the formfitting shirt I was wearing, with the V-neck that showed off a little cleavage. The makeup I had on—it'd been thick this morning, dark lines around my eyes, heavy mascara. I didn't know how much of it was left, now. But it was definitely feminine—or traditionally feminine. I personally thought determining someone's gender by the makeup they wore, or the clothes, or the things they liked, or the way they talked, was ridiculous and outdated. And I knew Bellamy was hot—and exceptionally masculine—with eyeliner on.

"You look girly enough to me," she said dryly.

"'Girly' is a concept I don't really subscribe to," I replied, just as dry, and she gave me a sharp look and a slow nod. "And it's not really about how I look. Although," I said, thoughtful, "I think they were pretty disappointed when I pierced my nose. And about my tattoo."

Cara tilted her head to the side. "I don't see any tattoos."

I grinned. "Maybe later." Out of the corner of my eye, I saw Zevi collapsing back against the couch cushions, consumed with laughter.

"Stop it, you psycho. I'm trying to woo a pretty girl, here." I glanced around for something to throw at him, but the nearest thing was a cymbal, and that seemed like a bad idea.

He laughed harder, then gasped for breath. "Woo when I'm not in the room."

Cara had started to giggle too—an actual giggle, or at least what I thought an actual giggle sounded like—and I grinned a little bit. I tried to straighten my mouth and keep it contained, but I couldn't quite.

Cara settled down and grabbed a pillow to hug to her. "So what did your parents want?" she asked when we'd all gotten ourselves more or less contained.

My eyes went right back down to the drum kit. All of these heads were junk. It'd be best if I could change them all out. But that would be silly, since I wouldn't be here for very long, and heads were expensive. Maybe if I tuned them as best I could, they wouldn't sound quite like whacking cardboard boxes. I reached for the first tom and set it in my lap. I had a drum key in my pocket. I didn't even have to wonder about it. It was always there.

I thought about all the heads I'd changed in my old basement, the one with the couch Zevi had puked on. I'd bought them all myself too. Cheap stuff until I could afford to save up for something better. It wasn't that my parents had refused to pay for them, or for my drum kits or sticks. It was that I'd never bothered to ask. I hadn't known if they'd say no, but I hadn't ever wanted to give them a chance.

"They wanted me . . . They wanted me to take ballet instead of running track. They wanted me to play violin instead of drums. Or not play at all. They wanted me to go to college here, live here. They definitely didn't want me to consider music as an actual career. Imagine how horrified they were when we signed our first record deal." I laughed, but it wasn't anything like the way Cara and Zevi had been laughing a minute before. It was dry and sad and sharp. "They thought I couldn't think for myself. And they wanted to think for me."

"And they still want to think for you?" Zevi asked. He was gentle about it this time, his voice soft, like he was reaching out to me.

I nodded. I kept staring at the drum in my lap, my hand moving around on the top of it, loosening all the lugs so I could tighten them again, one at a time, and make the tension on the head even. "Kind of. Yeah. Yes. They do." I smacked my hand down on the drum head, heard the hollow thump it made. A terrible noise to my ears. "I'm almost thirty fucking years old." I did glance up then. Cara and Zevi were both watching me. Zevi looked thoughtful. Cara's eyes were wide, and I figured that after tonight, I'd never see her again. Maybe that was best. "Almost thirty," I repeated. "You'd think I might have some of this figured out by now."

Zevi turned from me to Cara and then back again, and when I peeked at Cara, she was focused on the couch. She was running her fingers over the rough fabric like I was running my hand over the head of the drum. I was trying to feel the tension, trying to anchor myself in the familiarity of that, the comfort of it. I thought she was trying to disappear. I'd asked her over here to hang out with me and Zevi, and we'd ended up having a weird discussion about my parents and how I wasn't a fully functioning adult, even though I'd been an adult for quite a while. Great.

I took a breath, ready to . . . I wasn't even sure. Change the subject or apologize or get us out of this conversation somehow. Even Zevi seemed guilty. But then Cara started to talk.

"My parents kicked me out when I was eighteen. An adult. Technically." She glanced up at me and gave a half smile. Her fingers were still tracing around on the pilled surface of the couch. "I told them I liked girls, and they told me I should probably try to find my own way in the world. And for a long time, I thought it was my fault. My fault that they didn't want me anymore."

I felt immediately and horribly guilty. I hadn't been disowned. I didn't think I would be even if I told my parents I was bisexual. I hadn't been abused or abandoned. My parents loved me, and even when I doubted them, or didn't understand them, or wanted to shake them for the things I felt, I had never questioned that. I was one of the lucky ones.

Maybe she saw it on my face, because she held up her hand and leaned forward. I didn't think she remembered that Zevi was even in the room, she was so intent on me. She stared straight at me, and held my eyes, and I couldn't turn away.

"I'm not telling you to suck it up," she said firmly, her voice doing that thing that was the universal sound for *Don't argue with me*. "I'm not telling you that you shouldn't feel bad because you don't have it as bad as some people do. I think that's bullshit. I got dealt a hand, and you got dealt a hand, and they're both good and shitty in different ways. And they can't be measured against each other. They just can't. So stop thinking it."

I nodded automatically. "Okay."

On the other side of the couch, Zevi shifted in his seat. I didn't know if he was uncomfortable with this whole conversation—that *he* had started, intentionally or otherwise—or if he had something to add, and I almost didn't care. I didn't want to turn away from Cara. This was her and me, and her moment. Her hair was swinging in her face, the short strands almost covering her eyes, and there were two bright, nearly perfectly circular spots of red on her cheeks. But she didn't brush her hair aside, and she didn't lean back, either, and if her eyes were a little damp, I was willing to chalk it up to old anger. She was . . . beautiful. Breathtakingly beautiful. Like she was ablaze, all impassioned with what she was saying, what she wanted to tell me, and I was a tiny bit frightened to be at the center of that. But the rest of me kept reminding that nervous part how fucking lucky I was that she was looking at me like this. That she was showing me this piece of her.

"What I mean," she continued, her voice softer, not quite as hard, "is that . . ." she shrugged and glanced nervously over at Zevi, then back to me, "being an adult doesn't mean you automatically have it all figured out. It doesn't really mean anything, except that you get to vote. And that your parents can kick you out and there's nothing that can stop them. But it doesn't mean you have all the answers." Another glance at Zevi, and this time I thought she was trying to include him in the conversation. "Sometimes it takes a long time to figure that shit out. Took me a long time, at least."

I wasn't really sure what to say to that. I mean, I thought she was one hundred percent right, and logically, I'd known what she was saying was true before she said it. Hitting eighteen didn't prove anything, didn't make you an invincible adult. You didn't wake up one day and suddenly realize all the ways your parents screwed you over, or how your teenage friends messed you up. You didn't all of a sudden have everything about yourself or the people around you figured out.

But it felt like I should have, and I couldn't stop myself from thinking that. Part of me still wanted to let my parents think for me, because they were my parents, and I was the kid. And even though I'd spent most of my childhood and teenage years—and let's be real, my adult years—defying what they wanted from me, every time I did it, I was still . . . anxious about it. Because they were my parents and they should know best. And because all of my defying and rebelling and doing the opposite of what they wanted had never had anything to do with hurting them, or being stubborn, or proving something to them. It had only been about doing what I knew I needed to do to be happy. And I didn't want to disappoint them, even now.

"Takes all of us a long time," Zevi said into the silence that was growing in the room. "At least we're figuring it out though, right? Some people don't ever, I think. Don't ever know themselves well enough, outside of the box they've been given."

Cara pulled in a long, slow breath and leaned back against the couch cushions again. "True. I think they don't." She flashed a quick smile at me. "Least we're not living in a box."

"True," I repeated, and smiled back at her shyly. I wasn't a shy person, generally. But it was like we'd just shared something or walked through something important together, even if it was only something small, and I wasn't sure how to look at her, or myself, right now. But I knew I was glad she was here.

By the time Zevi left an hour later, I had the drum kit all set up, Zevi had told seven more embarrassing stories that'd made both me and Cara laugh until we cried, and Tuck had texted me three times. I hadn't read the texts—I figured they were probably jokes or about songs or something he found funny or interesting. That was how Tuck and I worked. We talked to each other all the time, any time, about whatever was on our minds. But I didn't want to interrupt my time with Cara and Zevi, not right now. I didn't want to think about how much I wanted to go home when I was actually, for the moment, pretty content. If it was something really important, Tuck would call.

The room had been full of laughter and conversation, and when Zevi left, it was like he took some of it with him. Not in a bad way. But it was quieter, and the room felt a bit closer with only me and Cara in it. She tipped sideways on the couch, lying down, and watched me while I sat behind the kit, making sure everything was positioned right, everything within reach, tapping the drums lightly with a stick. I didn't want to hit anything—it had gone quiet upstairs too, and I figured Mom and Dad had gone to bed—but I skimmed my sticks over the heads, testing reach, and tapped my feet against the bass pedal so it thumped softly.

I looked up from my testing and found Cara still staring at me, her eyelids heavy, like she might doze off. But she was focused on me, enough that I could feel it, and it made my heart pound a couple of times.

"How's it look?" I asked, softly. It seemed like conversation should be soft now—now that it was late, now that the house had gone to bed around us.

The grin on Cara's face this time was slow, and wide, and lovely, and a little bit flirty. "You know I have no idea what a drum set should look like, right?"

I smiled back. "Didn't ask if it looked right. Only how."

Her smile went impossibly wider, and she closed her eyes and pressed her cheek against the couch like she was embarrassed enough to want to hide her face. "Pretty sexy, honestly, you sitting behind it."

I swiveled around on the seat and came to sit in front of the couch. Cara's eyes were still closed.

"Yeah?"

Her smile flickered across her face again when I spoke, my voice so much closer to her now. But she didn't open her eyes.

"Yeah. I can picture you on stage. With your band."

I let my eyes wander over her, over her hair, falling across her cheek, catching the lamplight so it wasn't only that lovely brown, but a thousand shades of honey and dark. Her skin looked soft, delicate, but her body was strong. Her fingers were curled around the edge of the cushion, and I wanted to touch them, loosen that clasp, or make it tighter.

"Is it dark? Are the lights down on stage?" My voice was just a breath. I was afraid to break this spell.

"Mm-hmm." The sound caught in her throat, and I could see the blood rising to her cheeks, to the sharp angled dip at her collarbone. But she kept talking, and she kept letting me stare. She had to know that was what I was doing. I was close enough that she could probably feel my breath on her, but she didn't move away, and her eyes stayed closed. "Colored lights. Green and blue and purple. Lighting you up. Making that blond hair shine." She laughed a little to herself.

"Not a fan of the blond?" I asked, teasing. I gave in to what I wanted and ran a finger, very lightly, down the back of her hand. Her laughter stopped, her breath stuttering out in a tiny gasp. Her fingers fluttered, then closed even tighter on the cushion, like I'd been hoping for. I hesitated, then trailed my finger up to her wrist, around the curve of her bones, along the underside of her arm. I stopped when I got to her elbow, waiting for her to pull away, to tell me to stop. But she didn't. She was breathing hard, as if I'd touched her in a way far more intimate than dragging a finger along her skin. But I was breathing just as hard. And all my focus belonged to her.

I dragged my finger back down her arm, slowly, tracing the same path.

Her breath shuddered out in something that was almost a laugh, but not. Too shaky. "Oh no," she said, and her words were equally shaky. "I like the blond."

"Good." I was so absorbed in the sight of my fingers on her, moving along the slender bones of her knuckles, over the gentle curves of her fingernails, smooth under the tip of my finger, I almost forgot what we were talking about. "Where are you, while I'm on stage?"

She lifted her hand a fraction, and I slipped my hand into hers. Her fingers closed over mine, her thumb skimming along my palm. "I'm off to the side. The side of the stage, behind the curtain. You can see me if you look up."

She hadn't let my hand go, and I didn't want her to. I lifted my free one, brushed the hair back from her face. Smoothed my thumb over her cheekbone. Ran my fingertips down the side of her face, down her neck. I watched goose bumps rise up everywhere I touched, a tangible wake behind my fingers. It was possibly the most fascinating thing I'd ever seen.

"Do I look up?" I thought I'd forgotten to breathe. My voice sounded scraped raw, and the words came out in a breathy rush.

She opened her eyes then, and I looked down into them. She didn't blink or turn away, and I could feel myself get lost in her. I tried to remember the last time I'd looked at someone like that, looked at them like they mattered. The last time someone had held my gaze for more than a second. Tried to remember the last time I'd touched someone like I was touching Cara, touching her because I thought she was beautiful and I wanted to know what her skin felt like on mine. Because that was all there was, at that moment, to the need I had. I wanted to touch her, and I wanted her to touch me, and I wanted her to look at me with those clear eyes and *see me.*

She twisted her hand a little more, so our fingers were intertwined.

"You look up," she said, her eyes still on me. "You see me."

I forgot where we were, forgot everything else that had happened in the last few days, everything that would happen. Cara was all I could see and I wanted to keep it that way. "Then what?"

She pressed her lips together and shook her head, the tiniest movement against the cushion of the couch.

"What do you want to happen?" I asked her instead.

She tightened her fingers on mine, so hard it almost hurt, and I wanted more of it. "I want you to kiss me."

I leaned forward—I didn't even have to get up on my knees—and touched my lips to hers. Soft at first, and gentle like it had been when we'd kissed the night before. The start of something. But her free hand came up, her palm slipping around the back of my neck, her fingers burying themselves in my hair. She tugged and I moaned, my mouth opening against hers. There wasn't a single thing I could do about it, and I didn't want to do anything, anyway. I just wanted to keep kissing her.

Cara untangled our fingers and wrapped her other arm around me, sliding her hand up my back. Her palm was hot, even through the cotton of my T-shirt, and she pressed hard, urging me toward her, pulling me closer. I did kneel then, so I was hovering above her. She scooted over on the couch, her hands never quite leaving me, and I followed, until I was stretched out beside her. The couch wasn't made for lying side by side, and our bodies were squished together, but I was grateful for it. I wanted the feel of her all along me. Her knees pressed into my shins, her hip bones sharp against mine, her arm tucked between us, mine all tangled up with it so that if either of us moved, I suspected we'd probably injure each other. I didn't care how uncomfortable it could be, and apparently she didn't either, because she was kissing me again, harder than before, her tongue slipping between my lips so I could taste her. She tasted sweet, like sugar. Sugar and coffee and salt.

She slid her hand up my body, over my hip and up my waist, rucking up my shirt, her fingers finding skin. She moved her hand around my back, under my shirt, and tucked her fingers under the back of my bra. She didn't unhook it, didn't let her fingers wander, but when the bra tightened, that tiny bit, when she made room for herself there, my breath caught so hard I wasn't sure I'd be able to get it back. I thought of all the times I hadn't bothered to take my bra off at all, when my hookup's idea of touch was to push me back against the nearest wall and make enough room for them between my legs. Or the times when I'd unhooked it myself, shoved it over my shoulders so I could get a little touch, even if it was rough, or uncaring. And I'd wanted it, both of those ways—I'd always wanted it, and I hadn't regretted it. But this was different. This was intimate. It felt like Cara was touching me for the same reason I was touching her—because I wanted to know her. I wanted to know what she felt like when I held her against me. When she was happy.

And something about how good it was, that simple touch, something about how much it undid me, made me think we should stop. This wasn't right. She knew I was leaving soon. But she didn't know about Tuck. And it was ridiculous to dwell on that, when Tuck wasn't here and Cara probably wasn't planning on getting attached to me anyway, but I couldn't help it. I was getting attached. I could feel how easy it would be. And I felt like I was doing something wrong, even while I wanted to reach for her and hold her closer, press myself against her until I dissolved into her.

She must have felt me tense up or hesitate, because she pulled back, as far as my arms and the back of the couch would let her, and gazed at me. "Are you okay?"

I stared back at her. Her hands had slipped out of my shirt and come around, so she was holding my shoulders. Not pushing me away or pulling me closer, but holding me. So I couldn't run away maybe, or wouldn't. She was smiling, that tiny, private smile someone gives when they're happy and nervous and excited all at the same time. And she felt so solid and real, and she looked so hopeful.

I pulled in a breath, let it run through me.

"We don't . . . We can take it slower." She circled her hands over my shoulders, down my arms a little way. Soothing. I leaned in to her touch.

"It's not . . ." I laughed, even though this wasn't funny, and the sound that came out of me was hard and harsh and not really a laugh at all. I thought of all the times when things had been so much faster than this. So rushed that sometimes I didn't even really remember what happened, and I had to piece it together from little fragments after it was over. If I even bothered to do that. This wasn't about that at all.

I wanted to tell her something that would make sense. I didn't even know how to explain it to myself, though. She was looking less confused and more hurt with each second that I didn't say anything, and I knew I had to open my mouth and at least try to explain, but I couldn't. I couldn't find any words.

I didn't want her to look like that. I didn't want to put that expression on her face. And I didn't want to feel like that inside, either. We had been fine. Cara knew what the score was. She knew I was leaving, and that was enough.

My phone buzzed from where I'd left it on the floor. It made the same sound for everyone who texted me, but I knew, without having to check, that it was Tuck. And instead of the warm rush I usually got when he texted or called, a flicker of hot anger rose up in me. Why couldn't I just want what I wanted? Why did what I felt for him always have to be a ghost over everything?

I leaned forward and kissed Cara again. It took her a surprised second to decide whether she wanted to push me away or not. But she didn't. She melted back into it, and then we were kissing harder and deeper than before, that tiny flame of guilt and anger making me press closer instead of pulling back.

I couldn't get out of the trap I'd made for myself by falling for Tuck. I couldn't tell him, had never been able to tell him, because it might hurt the band. And I couldn't get myself away enough to deal with it, because he and Escaping Indigo were my life, and I wanted it that way. It ate me up inside, but I'd chosen it.

But what I could do was kiss Cara like that didn't matter, could pretend all of that wasn't going on in my head, could throw myself into her and hope I could forget for a while.

Cara went with it, matched my aggressiveness with her own. When I reached for the hem of her shirt, she caught my hands and reached down to pull it up and off herself, and then she reached for mine, so we were finally skin to skin. I'd forgotten how that felt. How the simple warmth of being touched fed a huge hunger that never quite abated.

Our hands tangled together, reaching for the same places on each other, the proximity the couch was forcing on us meaning we had to sneak fingers down stomachs, across chests, curve them around waists, so each touch felt desperate and lovely and intimate and stolen.

"Fast." Her voice was only a whisper in my ear. "This is fast. I'm sorry."

I almost laughed, because comparatively, this was as slow as it got for me. Those times before had been so different. They'd never had much tenderness. Too little caring, not enough sweetness. And this . . . this was fast, but it had so much of that it seemed almost overwhelming in how good it was, how lucky it made me feel.

And I almost apologized, because I was the one who'd pushed for fast, and I was the one who was still wondering if we should even be doing this now. But instead I shook my head, and she reached for me again, and we were unhooking bras, our hands getting all caught up in the straps, then reaching down for jean buttons and zippers.

I hesitated before I reached down any farther. My hand was cupped around her breast, her nipple a tight pebble against the palm of my hand, and that itself felt far more intimate than any quick and dirty thing I'd done in the past. But I wanted to be sure.

"Is this okay?" My voice was so breathy I wasn't sure she'd be able to make out the words.

She bit at her lip, leaving little crescent marks in the red. Then she smiled, shy but not unsure. "I want you." She gave a little shrug, a sharp roll of her shoulders that should have been ungraceful, but her body wouldn't move like that. Everything she did was fluid.

She kissed me again, then drew away enough that she could kiss down my neck, across my collarbone, into the hollow of my throat. It was incredible, her tongue so soft and light against my skin, the nearness of her a strange kind of intoxicating. She moved back up, and I took a second to stare at her. She was all smooth, tight muscles under sleek skin. Flat stomach, a gentle dip at her bellybutton. Plain black bra still hanging onto her shoulders, making her skin appear even paler. She looked strong and fragile at the same time, her shoulders slightly tense, thrown back, the lines of her collarbones and ribs divided by shadows. She didn't try to cover herself, or stop me looking, and I thought that was so brave.

I wasn't ashamed of my body. I was in shape from drumming, and the running I did when I was at home. But I wasn't particularly gorgeous, either. Not like Cara was. But when she pulled my bra aside, and undid my own jeans, I tried to lie still like she had. Tried not to hunch my shoulders or look down, or away. It was hard, though. My body worked for me. Moved in ways, with a precision, that few other bodies could. My mind made patterns and music, and my body turned it into sound and motion. But in front of Cara I was self-conscious. Ungainly, almost. She was taller, but she was so graceful, like light on water, lovely and slender and perfect. Everything about her—her small breasts, her long toes, the fine bones of her wrist—accentuated that. And I was just me. Not quite pretty. A little bit boring. Too short and too rough around the edges.

But Cara wasn't looking at me as if she saw me like that. She was looking at me like she couldn't take her eyes off me, like she wanted to take all of me in and didn't know where to start. She smoothed her hands over my chest, her fingers gentle and teasing, until I was panting and I forgot what my own hands were doing. She brushed her fingers over my waist, then up, along the undersides of my arms, making me shiver, over my shoulders, past my neck, burying them in my hair when she kissed me.

I dragged my hands down her chest, down across all the smooth skin, until I hit her jeans again. I'd gotten them undone, but now I tugged them down far enough over her hips that I could get a hand into her underwear. She was slick and hot, and I pressed against her, maybe a little too hard because I was so stupidly eager. But she gasped and arched against me, and my ego ratcheted up about ten notches.

She was scrabbling at my jeans, trying to yank them down, and I realized they were the skinny ones and probably too tight for rolling-around-on-the-couch-sex fun. I shimmied my hips and we spent a frantic few moments trying to get them off without my having to move the hand I had on her. Then her own fingers were pressing against me, stroking that perfect spot, and any laughter in me evaporated into moans. She was good at this. Her touch was just right, and she wrapped her other hand around the back of my neck, so as we arched and ground against each other, our foreheads bumped and our breaths came in hot puffs, and we kissed when we could get enough coordination to get our mouths together.

She came first, lifting her hips up, pressing hard against my palm, and I tried to keep it moving, to make it last for her. But then she was sneaking her own fingers down, a tiny bit at first, as if to see if I'd stop her, if I didn't want that. I spread my legs, and she slipped two fingers into me and pressed forward, firm, stroking, looking for the places that felt good, and I came so hard I thought my vision would go black.

When I drifted back to myself, we were a sticky, sweaty mess on the couch, but I didn't want to move. We were still pressed up against each other, her skin so hot on mine, and I wanted to stay that way. She'd moved her hand away, and she was resting it on my hip, her fingers drawing a little pattern there.

I smoothed my own hand down her waist. I felt amazing. Loose and languid and as if she'd completely taken me apart. But as the euphoria faded, the rest of the world started to crash back down, a piece at a time, like it was happening in slow motion.

Cara must have felt me . . . tense or pull away from her, even though I didn't actually move. She cleared her throat and tugged at her bra, covering herself again, and I sat up. The motion made it feel like a wall had come up between us. A minute before, I'd been more connected to her than I could remember being to anyone in . . . so long. And now I couldn't have reached for her if I tried.

We put our clothes back on, tugged up our jeans. I found a towel, and we wiped our hands on it. Cara brushed her hair back and put it up into a short ponytail, which started losing pieces almost immediately. And then we stood there, awkwardly, in the middle of the basement. I realized, with belated horror, that we hadn't locked the door, that we hadn't tried to be quiet. That my parents could have come down anytime, or that they might have heard us. The thought made me flush.

Cara saw it, and I didn't know what she thought it meant, but she ducked her head and looked embarrassed. It was the last thing I wanted her to feel. But I didn't know what to say. While I was struggling with it, my phone buzzed again. Tuck. It seemed like such a sign. He was between us and Cara didn't even know it. Would never know it. But it wasn't fair to her, either way. What we'd just done had been so . . . amazing and huge and weirdly important, even though it had been, truly, casual sex, like any other casual sex I'd ever had. Except it hadn't been.

"I should probably go to bed," I said. I wasn't sure if I was trying to make my voice sound easy, or whether I was giving her a clear sign to leave, and it came off somewhere in between. It wasn't the sweet goodbye I'd been hoping for a few minutes earlier, though, when I'd still been sky high, and by the way Cara's face fell, I knew it wasn't what she wanted either. But she only nodded. She grabbed her bag from the floor, took a step like she'd step toward me, but then shook her head and stopped.

"Call me?" She sounded too hopeful and too hurt.

"Yeah." It wasn't a promise, and we both knew it.

She walked to the stairs before I could go with her, and a second later, I heard the door shut behind her. I waited a minute before I followed to lock it.

chapter seven

I slept poorly, tossing and turning, my half-awake mind running over everything that had happened, everything that had been said, over and over. With my parents, with Cara. I'd glanced at my texts from Tuck—they were nothing important, little things to make me laugh, to make me feel like I was still part of him and Bellamy and the band, even though I was far away. Tuck wasn't the most thoughtful guy on the planet, and I was almost positive that Lissa might have had something to do with reminding him to call me, but he loved me, and I knew it. He cared about me and he wanted me to know he cared, and normally that would have made me feel so lucky. Now, however, it only hurt. Now it felt like a trap.

I stumbled down the stairs the next morning, almost more tired than when I'd gone to bed. I should have felt awesome. I'd gotten laid, Cara was gorgeous, and she wanted to see me again. But instead I only felt guilty. I hadn't told her the truth, even if it didn't really matter in the long run. And what I wanted was all tangled up in what I owed her, and Tuck, and I couldn't sort it out.

What I wanted right then, without thinking further than the next few minutes, was to get a cup of coffee and pour some caffeine into my system before I staggered into the shower. But both of my parents were sitting at the breakfast table. Mom was sipping her coffee, and Dad had a book flat on the table. Mom's eyebrows rose when she saw me, moving higher up her forehead than I personally thought eyebrows had any right to go. Dad glanced up from his book, then back at the toast he was eating with the other hand.

Mom cocked her head to the side. "Your hair looks like a rat's nest."

"Oh, fuck me sideways."

"Ava!"

She looked so completely scandalized that part of me wanted to laugh, but I was too tired to find enough humor. I closed my eyes and tipped my head back and begged for patience. I didn't have any of that to find, either.

I opened my eyes and stared right back at her. "I don't care what my hair's like, Mom. It's honestly probably one of the last things on my mind. I don't care if I look tired. Because I am tired." I inched my way across the kitchen and grabbed a mug. I wanted to cling to the coffee maker, but I was sane about it and just poured myself a cup. I glanced over my shoulder at my parents while I rummaged through the drawer for a spoon. "I'm so tired. I don't know what I'm doing. You really did a number on me last night, you know? All this stuff you want me to be, and you forget that I already am someone." I almost told them, then, all of it. How they'd smothered me. How I'd met a gorgeous girl and I was fucking it all up because I couldn't even manage to fall in love like a normal person. Because I'd chosen to fall in love with the man who had made me who I was, and now there wasn't any way for me to undo that, despite how I wanted to *so badly*. How I wanted to go home, because it was the only place that I felt safe, but somewhere between yesterday and today, I'd started dreading it. Had started dreading seeing Tuck again, seeing the hole I'd created for myself by loving him, and not being able to do anything about it.

I stuck the spoon in my mug and stirred, vigorously enough that coffee spattered on the countertop. I turned around, the spoon still in my hand, and waved it through the air. I thought I saw my mother flinch, and somewhere in the back of my mind I realized I was probably still flinging coffee around her immaculate kitchen. My mother's mouth was hanging open. I didn't think I'd ever seen her quite so speechless, not like this. It should have been hilarious. It wasn't, though, and it made me shut my mouth instead of saying whatever I'd been about to. I wasn't even sure.

My dad closed his book, the movement careful, deliberate, and he pushed his coffee cup a little away. "We only want you to be happy."

I bit my lip. "I know. I really do know that. That's what makes it so . . . terrible. You have no idea what makes me happy. You've never known. You've never bothered to find out."

I didn't wait for him to respond, or for my mom to shut her mouth and pull herself together. I felt awful that I'd said anything at all. I hadn't meant to. I'd just been too tired to hold it in. But the expressions on their faces told me I should have tried harder. I turned and hurried up the stairs, my coffee clutched between my hands, careful so I wouldn't spill any of it. I shut my door behind me and slumped down against it. And then, while I drank my coffee, I couldn't stop myself from inching my hand up to my hair, to feel how bad it might actually look. To know what my mother had seen.

The next time I came down the stairs, showered and dressed and ready to go, there wasn't anyone there. We'd planned to all go over to my grandmother's house together, but when I poked my head into the garage, I saw that my dad's car was already gone. I didn't know if my mom was still here, or if she'd gone with him, and I didn't stop to find out. I grabbed my own keys off the counter and headed out.

When I got to my grandmother's house, I could hear people upstairs moving around. Zevi and my dad at least, and maybe my mom, and I didn't want to have to see or talk to any of them. Not even Zevi. Not right now. I snuck past the stairs as fast as I could, hoping no one would come down and catch me, and when I got to Gran's room, I shut the door behind me and slumped against it.

She was sitting in her chair, sorting through her clothes, and she looked up at me, then at the door, and raised her eyebrows. The gesture was so like my mother's and so not that it startled me. Curious where my mother's had been all demanding. But the type of curiosity I knew I wasn't supposed to ignore.

My grandmother had never been someone I'd gone to for help. She wasn't squishy hugs and cupcakes, although she did make a pretty fantastic peanut butter cookie. She wasn't the person you went to when you needed sympathy, because she was more likely to tell you what you should do about your problems—another way she was like my mom. But she was good at listening too. And maybe that was all I really wanted. Someone to listen to me.

I raised my hand and shoved it through my hair. *Not so rat's nest-like now, huh, Mom?* It fell through my fingers to swing at my chin, and when I shook my head a little, I could feel the cut edges of it against my skin.

"I had a . . . thing, with my parents. This morning." I waved my hand through the air. I wasn't sure if I was trying to describe how bad it was with the gesture, or make it seem like it was fine.

"What kind of thing?"

"Um." I didn't want to tell her. I didn't want to tell anyone, because I knew it would sound ridiculous. It was no big deal to anyone except me. And I didn't want to tell her about Cara yet, either. Maybe ever. But definitely not this morning.

Before I could answer, my grandmother held up her hand. "Never mind. I dare say it's been a long time coming. I know your mother. I know how she can get under people's skin. And I've been watching her get under yours for years. I'm surprised it took you this long to snap."

I blinked. "Really?"

She gave a tiny shrug, then swept her hand at the books. "Come read. It'll make you feel better to be lost in books."

I couldn't really argue with that, and I really didn't want to talk anymore anyway. I found a bare patch of floor and settled myself on it, and went to work. It was already starting to feel familiar and comfortable, my hands on the books, their words and covers floating in front of my eyes, the inky, dusty smell of them, the soft noises my grandmother made as she moved around her room. It was a bubble, and I knew that, but I was happy to be in it.

We worked in silence. I'd have liked to turn on the radio or something—I wasn't used to doing anything without music, but I didn't think Gran and I would share the same opinions on what songs were good. Instead, I let myself get absorbed in reading the back blurbs of the books. If I was really interested in something, then I'd ask her, and break the quiet in the best way.

Someone, probably Zevi, had pulled down the last of the books and piled them on the floor. I reached for a couple of stacks that were new to me, books I hadn't seen before. Most of them were by the same author, and I started reading the blurbs. They were fascinating, some kind of weird fairy tales for adults. I was about to ask my grandmother about one when I read past the blurb to the author bio.

There was something familiar about it. The way the author was described, the way the words jumped at me from the back cover. It felt like something I should know. And then I got to the part where the author's school and work history was described, and it clicked.

I held the book up to my grandmother, and she stared back at me, waiting for me to ask about it, like I had with every other book. But I didn't.

"This is you." I flipped the book around and tapped the back. She didn't say anything, just kept waiting. "This bio, this is you. I'm right, aren't I?"

It took her a long time to answer. I didn't think she was contemplating lying to me. I think I had, honestly, and maybe for the first time ever, caught her without anything to say.

Then she nodded, once. "It's me."

"You wrote these?" I had to be sure. It seemed so impossible. I didn't know why—anything was possible. But I felt like I should have known. All this time, growing up with her, spending all this time with her books, the books she loved, and the thought had never occurred to me.

"Yes." Her voice was a little more wry now. She pointed at a stack near my right knee. "Those too, I think. I'm not sure where Zevi put everything."

I lowered the book slowly. Part of me wanted to keep staring at it. It was a pen name on the cover, obviously, but the more I looked at it, the more I saw it as something my grandmother had picked to go on a book she'd written. It was a strange and amazing and slightly uncomfortable feeling.

"Were you going to tell me?" I turned to the other piles of books. Different titles. She'd written *a lot*. "Or were you going to let me ask you about them, and not tell me they were yours? Would I ever have known?"

She gave a little sigh. I thought she was trying to sound exasperated. But there was something else behind it. Some nervousness that wasn't quite guilt and wasn't really embarrassment. Suddenly, it occurred to me, what I had done. She'd had this secret, for however long—years, it must have been—and she had let me blunder into it. And I had. I'd ripped it open like it was my business to do. But I couldn't help being angry about it. Or . . . maybe hurt was the better word.

"You'd have known eventually," she said.

"So you weren't going to tell me," I pushed.

She raised her hands, then let them drop back into her lap. "I don't know, Ava. I didn't know what I was going to do. I hadn't decided."

I looked down at the book in my lap, ran my finger over the glossy cover, the name and title slightly embossed. Then I looked back up at her. "You asked me to help you. Me. You had to know I'd at least see them."

She nodded. Her fingers kept picking through her clothes, tossing stuff in one pile or another. We'd been at this for days. It seemed like it should take less time, to clean out a house, to pack up someone's stuff and move it here or there. But my grandmother had lived in this house for decades, with my grandfather, and then with another man, Henry, who I'd known even better than my real grandfather, and then, when Henry passed away, by herself. There were lifetimes in this house. Loves and losses, and even though it didn't seem like a lot, it was. And Gran was being asked to sort through and decide what she wanted. I was willing to give her as much time as we had.

But I hadn't ever expected to have a conversation that went like this with her.

"Yes." She glanced down, then back at me, and I couldn't quite tell, but I thought she was blushing. A hint of color, high on her cheeks, almost hidden by the gray and black hair she was letting fall in front of her face. "Ava. Do you remember when you came in here and told me why you understood about how I loved my books? Because you loved your drums the same way?"

I nodded. It had only been a few days ago. It wasn't like I was going to forget so soon.

"That's why I asked you. You and I are alike. Not in most ways. But in some."

My brows were pinching together, and my throat was suspiciously tight. This was the wrong time to see my grandmother as anything more than a figure in my life. To see her as a person in her own right.

Because this was the beginning of the end, and we could sugarcoat it however we liked, but we both knew it. She was failing and I lived across the country, and I didn't want her to be anything more than she'd always been, because it would make it so much worse. It would mean I was losing something I hadn't even known to look for.

"And Zevi?" I asked.

"I love Zevi," she said, more bluntly than I'd expected. But that was how affection was with her. Something that simply *was*. "But he hasn't found that thing to hold on to like you hold on to your music. Or I hold on to my words."

She watched me while I stared down at the books around me, seeing them differently now. Not only the ones Gran had written, but all of them. I hadn't really believed her, before, when she'd said these books were her life. But maybe they were. Maybe this was her heart.

"Don't get sentimental," Gran said, like she was reading my mind.

I took a deep breath. This was too much to take in, all at once. I didn't know how I was supposed to be feeling. If I should let everything be like it always had been. If that was even possible.

"Why did you keep it a secret?" I asked her.

She shrugged, and her lips twitched up into something like a smile. "I think . . . I wanted something that was only mine. A piece of me, for myself." She glanced at the door, then back at the books. "Some people knew. But not many."

That made sense. And . . . it didn't. These were published. It was obvious that other people had read them, and since she'd been published over and over, I was willing to bet at least someone had liked them. These books had gone out into the world. They hadn't been only Gran's at all.

"Ava," she said softly, pulling me out of my thoughts. "We're not done. We have a lot to do."

I nodded, more to shake myself out of my thoughts than anything. I started piling the books she'd written into a box.

"Are you taking those?" she asked.

"I'm taking them all." I looked up at her and found her staring at my hands, at the books disappearing into the box that would take them across the country. "Except the ones you want to keep," I said, more gently. "I'm taking them all."

She nodded. Then she pointed at one of the books she'd written, waiting in another pile. "Not that one. I want that one. For now."

I pulled it out and set it aside for her. I wanted to ask her about it, ask why that one in particular. But I didn't. Something about the way she looked at it made me think that, out of all of them, maybe that one held the biggest part of her heart. Maybe that one was the one that was, in some way, the most hers.

We went back to the way we'd been doing things before. I didn't ask her about her books, except for once more, when a particular title caught my eye. "I'll write you something about them," she said, "and send it." And that was the end of that discussion. I boxed them all up and labeled them to go to Tuck's house, since, if I shipped them soon, they might get home before I did. He'd keep them for me until I got back. I asked her about other books, and stacked them in boxes—I was getting awfully good at it. Those books weren't going to move around at all when they did get shipped. And by the time I stopped that evening and looked around, I realized I was mostly done. There were a few more stacks to go through, but my grandmother waved her hand at them and commanded that we do them tomorrow.

Zevi was still upstairs, and I went and called him down, and the three of us had dinner together, Chinese takeout that Gran made us dump out of the takeout boxes and onto plates so it would look like we were "at least trying." Then Zevi wondered out loud if Gran would still be able to order Chinese when she was at the assisted living, and she told him, straight-faced, that she'd order any damn thing she pleased. And I laughed so hard I think I startled them both.

Later, when we were standing in the driveway getting ready to go, Zevi asked me if I wanted to go out, maybe catch a local show or a movie or something, but I shook my head and promised him tomorrow instead. I was in a weird mood, and I wasn't sure what I wanted or needed, but I didn't think I'd be very good company.

I hopped in my car, watched Zevi leave, and then I found myself driving again, like I'd been doing since I got here.

I kept getting distracted by the trees. They were so much bigger and taller than I remembered them—they seemed that way every time I came back. And I'd toured the country, but we'd stayed on highways and in cities, for the most part. This town, the surrounding area, was by no means as rural as it got—the city was less than an hour away—but it was different than where we'd been. Or maybe I was just seeing it more, because it had been mine once. And these trees . . . They closed everything off. Made everything appear like it was covered in green. There were a lot of things I wasn't happy about where I lived now, but I could see the sky. I could watch the clouds coming in and see the sunset and the stars. There wasn't anything in the way of that. I didn't think I'd ever want to trade those summer storms, watching the thunderheads building, for tall trees again.

I found myself, once it was almost dark, driving down the street where Cara's dance studio was. I wanted to be surprised with myself, but I wasn't. Annoyed, yeah, definitely. I could have called Tuck again, or Bellamy or Micah, instead of going to find Cara. But I wanted to avoid them for the moment, because I was afraid they might hear how twisted up inside I was. I'd thought about avoiding Cara for the same reason. Putting all of this behind me and pretending it hadn't happened. Maybe that would be easiest. But Cara deserved more than that.

I'd told Cara I'd see her again, but seeing her again wasn't the same as dropping in on her where she worked. It wasn't quite stalker material, but it wasn't really something you were supposed to do, either. I knew I should probably keep driving, go back to my parents' place, and call Cara instead. But I didn't want to go home. I'd managed to avoid my parents all day, and I wanted to keep doing it. And I wanted to see Cara. Just for a minute.

I parked a little way down the street and got out to walk. It was warm out, an evening breeze creating the tiniest chill. I was slightly dusty and sweaty from working all day, and the breeze felt good on my skin. Felt almost like being home, and I wanted to stand in it and soak up that feeling.

Cara's dance studio had a huge front window that looked into a big open rehearsal room. The lights were on, and it was easy to see inside. That was the purpose, I supposed—to tempt people with the honey shine of the hardwood floor, the elegance of the bar set against mirrors at one side of the room. To show what you could do with your body, to let people stare at the dancers as they moved, graceful and beautiful and a little bit wild.

Cara was there, in the center of the room. There were a couple of other people too, and it seemed like they were practicing a routine—the things I knew about dance could fill a thimble—but she stood out for me. Of course she did. She was lovely. But there was something about the way she moved, something about the energy she held inside, like she coiled it up in her, waiting for the exact right time to use it, that made her glow. She would have drawn my eye even if she weren't gorgeous. If she were on stage, performing, I wouldn't have been able to turn away, and I was willing to bet a lot of other people saw the same thing in her.

As it was, it seemed that she was only practicing, maybe working on a single section of a routine. She and the other two dancers performed the same move over and over, sometimes spilling over into other moves afterward. The other dancers were good too, but I couldn't pull my gaze away from Cara. Any elegance or grace I'd seen in her movements up until now was, I realized, a shadow of this. It was like I'd only seen her at half speed before. Now she was *alive*.

Cara couldn't hold on to drums like I could, or books like my gran, but I knew while I was watching her that it was the same for her. That this was the thing that was central to her. That made her who she was.

I didn't know how long I stood there, staring. People passing by probably wondered what the hell I was doing. I didn't care. I wasn't even really thinking about it. All I was thinking about, for those few minutes, was Cara. No Gran, no parents, no Tuck. Only her and the way she danced across the floor.

One of the other dancers glanced at me, once, through the window, but other than that, they didn't look my way. I wondered if they were so used to being watched they didn't care anymore, or if they'd trained themselves to pretend the window wasn't there. It didn't matter. I didn't know if I wanted Cara to see me or not. I couldn't decide, and I didn't want to have to. I only wanted to stand there and ache for her. It was simple like this.

They wrapped up eventually. They stood there and smiled and talked, and then they all went to the corner of the room for their bags, towels, and water bottles. That was my chance to go and not let her know I'd been there at all, but I couldn't make myself move.

And when she stood up again, Cara stared straight at the window, straight at me. Maybe she'd known I was there the whole time.

She held up a hand, palm out, then folded her fingers down until she only held up one. *Wait.* And there wasn't any way I could go anywhere after that.

It didn't take her long—she came out with the tips of her hair slightly damp, as if she'd just washed her face. She had pulled a jacket on and changed into jeans. She smelled of plain soap and sweat, and it took pretty much everything I had in me not to reach out for her. Tuck would be proud of my restraint. If he were here, he'd probably be laughing his ass off at how badly I was screwing all of this up.

The thought of him was comforting and sobering in equal measures. I sighed, and Cara's shoulders slumped a little, so the small duffel bag she had in her hand brushed against the concrete.

"What are you doing here, Ava?"

I pressed my lips together and shook my head slowly, and then a little faster. "I don't know."

She hoisted the bag up onto her shoulder. "I'm glad for it." She was blushing and smiling, a little shy and a lot unsure. "I thought, after last night . . . I thought I might not see you again."

"Yeah?" I was hopeful and nervous and guilty, all at the same time, and I didn't know what to do about any of it.

She nodded. She looked as uncertain as I felt, and I hated that I'd done that to her, today, and last night. "What are you doing here?" she asked, almost gently.

"Um." What *was* I doing here? I'd wanted to push her away, and then I'd found out about my grandmother's books, and I'd come here and spied on Cara through a window. It was all messed up. What I'd wanted was a friendly face. What I'd wanted was to see her again and have her tell me . . . that things were okay. That I hadn't screwed everything up with everyone. But I shouldn't have been here at all, because nothing had changed.

"I . . ." I started, then stopped and tried again. "I'm going through my grandmother's books." Because obviously this was the time for that. What was wrong with me?

"Okay." She drew the word out a little, but she sounded like she was ready to listen to whatever I had to say.

"She wrote them," I blurted. "Not all of them. Obviously," I added quickly, but then I realized it didn't matter because I hadn't told Cara about the books before. She didn't know how many there were. She didn't know anything about this. "Some of them. Under a pen name. It was like she had this . . . I think she had this whole secret life. Separate from . . . everything. From me and Zevi. From my mom." I wondered, then, for the first time, if my grandfather had known. He must have. Surely she would have told him. But my parents? My aunt? My grandmother's friends? I had no idea. I didn't know about any of this either. I didn't know why I was telling Cara, even, or what I was trying to say.

She reached out and touched the tip of her finger to my hand, drawing my thoughts back to her, back to right now. "You didn't know?"

I bit my lip and shook my head, and suddenly, out of what felt like nowhere, I thought I might cry. Gran was her own person. She was an adult who had had a life before me, and would have one when I went home. She could keep all the secrets she wanted. But this felt, somehow, like a betrayal. I'd thought I'd known her, known who she was, all this time, and now I knew I was wrong. Or, at least, not quite right. And I couldn't get those two things, those two pieces of her, to mesh in my mind.

"I want to go home," I told Cara. This was bad. This was not the type of thing you told someone when you wanted them to like you. This was needy and pathetic, but I couldn't make it stop. "I don't want to be caught up in any of this anymore. I want to go home and pretend it's not happening."

"Is that what you do?" she asked. I stared at her, but her words had been gentle. Not angry. Not like she was chiding me for something. Only . . . curious. "You go home and try to forget about what's here? Forget about what's happening with your family?"

"My family is across the country."

She nodded. "I get that." A sharp, sad smile flickered over her face. "But I think that if that were one hundred percent true, you wouldn't be so shaken up about what's been going on since you got here. It wouldn't bother you so much."

"I . . ."

She took my hand then and tugged so I'd start walking. "Come on. Come, um . . . Let's sit down or something. We don't have to talk about this in the middle of the sidewalk."

She led me to her car, and unlocked it so we could get in. She slung her bag into the back, then came around and sat in the driver's seat. She rolled down the windows and moved her seat back, then turned so she could face me.

"Start again."

I huffed out a laugh. "I don't know where to start. I don't know what I'm doing here. Everything is different . . ."

"This isn't the first time you've been back, is it?"

I shook my head. "Longest visit, though, in a long time." I waved my hand through the air. "I don't know what happened. It's like whoever I was, when I was here, the last pieces of that person are gone."

"Is that a bad thing?"

I focused on the dash so I wouldn't have to meet her eyes. "I don't know. I don't think so. But it hurts."

She was quiet for a minute, letting that sink in. "Ava," she said finally, "why did you come to find me today?"

I swallowed and made myself look up. She was leaning toward me, the smallest bit, but she looked like she was ready to lean back, put a wall between us, if she had to.

"Why did you let me sleep on the plane?" I asked her back. "Why were you kind?"

She let out a slow breath. "You smiled at me when I sat down."

"That's it?"

She shrugged. "You looked at me like . . ." She copied my hand movement, swishing hers through the air like she could pluck the right words out of it. But she didn't say anything else. She watched me and waited for me to say something instead.

I sighed. "I like you, Cara." I wanted to reach out again. I wanted to feel her against me like I had the night before. It seemed like more time had passed than that. Too much time since she'd touched me, since I'd felt her hands on me. I hadn't realized how much I missed that, how much need I had for a touch that was about me and the other person and not whatever was going to happen between us.

Just *us*. A need, a kind of loneliness, that I'd been pushing aside for so long, I'd forgotten it was really there.

But now that need was wide-awake and angry, and I couldn't do anything about it.

She leaned the tiniest bit closer to me, and I wanted to move forward and kiss her and let that solve everything, stop all the conversation and the thoughts in my head, like it had last night. But she spoke before I could.

"Ava. What happened last night? I thought . . ." She blushed and dropped her gaze, and something in my heart gave a sharp, stinging twist. "I thought we were . . . It was so good. And I like you. And I thought . . ."

This was why I couldn't kiss her and solve things that way. This was why I shouldn't have done it the night before. "I'm going home. This . . ." I raised my hand, then let it fall right back in my lap. "This isn't going to work."

"I'm not asking for it to work," she said, her words hard. "I'm not asking you to fall in love with me in a week. I'm asking . . . Don't you feel like we might . . . have something?" She was looking at me again, and she seemed so hopeful. So nervous and hopeful, almost like she had when she first sat down beside me on the plane, only so much more. "We could . . . We could try—"

I shook my head before she could say anything else. "No. It's not fair."

She tucked her chin in, as if surprised. "Not fair to who?"

"To all of us." That was a mistake. Tuck was on my mind, but I hadn't mentioned him to Cara at all. "To you or me. It's not . . . I can't ask you that."

"You're not." Then she stopped and thought about what I'd said. "Do you think it's not fair of me to ask you?"

I didn't. I was thrilled and confused, and I wanted her to keep asking me until I said yes. But there was Tuck and the band and my parents and this place, and I couldn't see a way around any of it.

"Why are you here?" she asked again, and this time there wasn't anything gentle in her voice. "Why are you here, telling me all of this?" She narrowed her eyes at me. Her expression was hard, her jaw set. It wasn't an expression I'd ever have pictured on her face, but she pulled it off startlingly well. It wasn't something I ever wanted aimed at me again. "Are you breaking up with me?"

The question took me by surprise, and I said the first thing that came to mind. "We're not really together to begin with." It was the truth—we'd known each other for less than a week. Dating wasn't what we were doing.

That didn't mean it was the best thing to say right then, though.

Cara sat back, like I was, so we were both pressed against opposite sides of the car. A spare part of my mind told me we must have looked ridiculous to anyone passing by. As if there were a giant spider between us on the console or something, and we were leaning away from it. It almost felt like that, with the tension balled between us.

"You have to go." Cara sounded so calm. Like it was an idea that had just occurred to her, and she was testing it.

I opened my mouth, closed it. I thought I knew what she was saying. But it wasn't quite adding up in my brain. "Go?"

"Go." She nodded, at me and at herself, I thought. "That's what you wanted, right? You came here and told me that you were leaving anyway, and that what we did last night was a mistake. Right? So go."

"That wasn't what I meant about last night." It hadn't been at all. Last night had been everything good I'd ever wanted sex to be, even though it had happened on a couch two floors below my parents, which, when I thought about it, was awkward as fuck.

"I don't care." Her voice wasn't simply firm now. It was hard, rock solid and with an edge to it that made me want to flinch. Sharp and immoveable. "I want you to go. Now. Get out."

I swallowed nervously. I hesitated for a second, and her eyebrows rose, her eyes going wide. I grabbed for the door latch. My hands were shaking, and I couldn't get a grip on it, but I didn't think Cara really cared to be patient with me, right then. I got the door open and stepped out, closing it behind me. I turned around, but she wasn't looking at me anymore. Her hands were planted firmly on the steering wheel. She stared straight ahead. I waited another few seconds, but she didn't move, and she didn't look away.

I couldn't stand there, in the street, and wait. I didn't know what to wait for, even. And I didn't think it would do any good. Cara was right. This was what I had wanted. I had felt so terribly guilty for leading her on, and I'd wanted to stop. And now I had. We had. I tried to remind myself of that, over and over.

I took a step, then turned and walked to my car. Cara's was behind me, and I couldn't help glancing back a couple of times, but she never looked up, never looked my way. When I got in my own driver's seat, I looked one more time, and saw that her car was gone.

chapter eight

I felt like the day had punched me in the stomach. It was pretty obvious I wasn't processing my feelings like a grown adult should, but when had I ever done that? I wanted to get in the house, maybe get something to eat, and then plant myself facedown on my bed and just lie there. It seemed like a pretty damn good plan.

When I stepped into the kitchen, though, my mom was there. She was sitting at the table, her hands folded neatly on the tabletop. She had a mug of tea, the tea bag still in it, in front her, but it looked like she'd only sipped at it. It looked, actually, quite a bit like she'd been waiting for me to get home. She sat up straighter when she saw me, and I thought I saw her tighten her hands, so her knuckles went pale, then flooded with color again when she released them.

She seemed . . . nervous and maybe even hopeful, and she opened her mouth as if she was about to say something. But I was frustrated and I felt guilty and awful and tired of feeling that way. And I didn't want whatever she said to hurt me. I didn't want to let it. And I knew so well it could.

I held up my hand before she could say a single word. I wanted to slump against the wall, maybe let myself slide all the way down to the floor. But I couldn't do that. I had to stand up straight.

"I found Gran's books," I said, and I knew, without having to say another word, that she knew exactly what I meant by that. Her face went so pale, milky, washed-out white. I'd heard the phrase *I saw the color drain* before, but I didn't think I'd ever actually seen it happen. "Her books," I pressed anyway. I wanted . . . I wanted to hurt her before she could get her thumb back over me. Even while I did it,

I knew it was childish, but I couldn't stop myself. "The ones she wrote. You knew, right?"

She was gaping at me, her mouth opening, then closing again, as if she couldn't find the words.

"I know you did." I hadn't been certain before. But now I was.

She shook her head, slowly. "It wasn't my secret to tell."

I jerked my head forward in a nod. "I get that." I did, too. I understood loyalty. I wasn't sure it made me feel any better, though.

My mother let out a harsh little laugh. "Those books. She loved those things more than anything."

"Wait . . . what?" She sounded so . . . derisive. Affronted, almost. Enough that it was surprising, the venom in her voice.

"Writing those things was her life." She looked up at me, and I got it. I actually got it. All this time, I'd let her and my father attempt to control me and direct me, and I'd fought against it, but I'd never wondered *why*. I'd never stopped to question what they were so afraid of.

"Is that . . ." I took a step forward. "Is that what you thought would happen? You didn't want me to be like her? Is that it?"

She was already shaking her head. "No. Ava. We wanted you to be happy."

"And you assumed you knew what would make me happy, right? Being normal? Not . . . not doing something I loved?"

She slapped her hand down on the table, and the sound was sharp enough that I jumped. I could feel my pulse in my throat. "I watched her let the writing rule her," she said, loud enough that she was almost yelling. I took that step backward again, but she was leaning forward, almost rising up out of her chair. "I watched her go through . . ." another sharp bark of laughter that told me she didn't find any of this funny at all, "depression and anxiety. So much stress. So much worry. Loneliness, even though she had us. All for those books." She was breathing hard when she was done throwing out the words. She sat back a tiny bit, but she was still humming with energy, like she was ready to start yelling again, if that's what she thought it would take, to make me understand. "And what did she get for it?" she asked, but she wasn't asking me. "What did she get? I didn't want that for you. I . . . I wanted things to be easy for you."

It was me who was at a loss for words now. My lower lip might have been trembling. This was too much, on top of everything else, and I didn't know how to respond to it. "She was happy," I said finally.

My voice sounded so small, but my mother acted like I had slapped her. She slumped against the chair. Her hand reached out, scrabbling for purchase, until she found the back of it, so she could hold on. Maybe so she could hold herself up. She stared at me, not as pale anymore. She'd flushed when she'd been shouting, and now bright pink streaked over her cheekbones, made her look angry and confused and shocked.

"She was happy," I said again, as much to myself as my mother. "I've seen her with those books. I've seen . . . They made her happy."

My mother swallowed, hard enough that I saw her throat move with it. A convulsive thing, like she was choking. "We could have made her happy."

I nodded. I could argue it, or agree and try to explain. Because it wasn't one or the other. It wasn't like that. But she didn't know that. So instead, I told her, "I've been happy."

She blinked up at me.

"Do you know that? All those times we were broke or rejected or no one wanted to let us play, all those times we thought we wouldn't make it. They were worth it. I've been happy. This has made me happy. It's made me . . ." I sighed and waved my hand around, trying to find a way to explain it.

Had she ever had anything like that? A passion so huge she couldn't ignore it, even when it felt like it might kill her? Something that was as much her life as breathing? Something that was completely intrinsic to her? I wanted to think it had been me, but I wasn't quite that selfish, not yet. And I didn't know the answer. I took a deep breath, letting my lungs expand, feeling the stretch of all that air inside me.

"It's made me feel so full," I told her. "Like I could overflow with all of it." Tuck would laugh at me for that, probably, and Bellamy too—he had a way with words, and that was why he wrote the lyrics and I didn't. But the explanation felt right to me, even if it was overly dramatic and too sentimental. At least it was honest.

And, almost as suddenly, I felt like I had overflowed. Like all the anger I'd had, everything I'd been wanting to say to my mother for so long, nearly didn't matter anymore. I just wanted it to stop. A clean break, if I could get one. But a break, one way or another.

"I've been able to be myself," I told her, and then I realized that wasn't quite true. I hadn't quite done that, because I'd been hiding. Because I'd been afraid. Because I'd always let Tuck, or Bellamy, or even Quinn, take the lead from me. Because I hadn't told Tuck everything I wanted to tell him. And because even though I'd moved away from my parents and tried to put their influence out of my mind, I'd still been worried about disappointing them. Maybe that would never go away. Maybe it would always be in the back of my mind. But I wasn't going to change what I was doing, either, or who I was, to make them feel better. I loved drumming. I loved being in Escaping Indigo. And I wanted to be able to be myself, be honest about who I was, in every aspect.

Might as well put it all out there now, while my mom was already upset with me. "I'm bisexual," I told her. She went, if possible, even paler. "I feel like a fraud, saying it," I admitted, and I gave a little shrug. At myself or for her, I didn't know. "I definitely lean in one direction. I'm always afraid someone's going to . . . I don't know. Call me out on it. Tell me I'm faking. Taking something that doesn't belong to me." I blinked, and I found that my eyes were a little damp. I was too wound up for this conversation. I'd started it, though, and now I wanted it out. "I could pass as straight and maybe it wouldn't ever make a difference, because I'm mostly attracted to guys. I could probably keep it hidden, and no one would ever know. Maybe it won't ever make a difference." I thought of Cara, for a flash. Her smile in my mind's eye. I didn't think I'd ever see her again. But still. "It makes a difference to me." It did, I realized. This was my mother. Above everything else, I wanted her to understand. I wanted her to tell me that she loved me.

"It does belong to me," I said. "Even if I never date another girl. Even if it never happens again. It's still who I am. The same way the music is who I am. I don't want to take that out of my life, Mom. None of it. Not the touring, not the recording, not the . . ." I laughed, "not the parts that make me stressed or depressed or angry or worried. I want all of it. It makes my life . . ." I shook my head. "It makes it worth something. For me. It lets me be me. Can you understand that?"

For a long minute, she didn't move. I imagined I could hear every sound magnified in that silence—the refrigerator running and the clock in the kitchen and the breath moving through me. I didn't think she was going to move at all, didn't think she'd say anything, and I didn't know what I'd do. But then she nodded, stiffly, once. And that was enough for me, for now. It was enough.

I nodded back and turned before either of us could say anything else. I needed it to stop there.

I went up to the guest room and shut the door behind me. I couldn't sit down, couldn't do anything. My mind was racing, and I paced back and forth, from the window to the door. Outside, the neighborhood looked like it always did, picture-perfect even after dark: mellow porch lights casting deep shadows on neat flower beds, the few streetlamps illuminating the road for the last couple kids, out on bikes, returning home. But inside, in this room, in my own mind, it was like everything had changed all at once, without any planning from me. I didn't know how to put it back together. I didn't know if I wanted to put it back together.

I pulled my phone out of my pocket and called up the text conversation Tuck and I had been having.

I'm bi, I typed, and hit Send before I could think any more about it, or wonder whether he'd even know what I meant, what I was talking about.

His reply came fast, maybe only a minute later. As if he'd typed without thinking, like I had, and just as quickly. *I know.* And, a second later, another text shook the phone in my hand, popping up over the first. *I love you.*

That's what I had wanted. It seemed so stupid, that I'd been afraid to voice it before now. Afraid to tell him. Afraid to tell anyone. But Tuck especially. I wasn't in love with him for no reason. He wasn't my best friend, the person I trusted most in the world, for no reason. I knew he didn't mean he loved me in the way I loved him. But he did love me, and that was what I'd wanted to hear. Needed to know. Even though it was ridiculous. I'd only wanted him, or anyone, to tell me that it was okay.

I flopped down on my bed and stared up at the ceiling. I didn't write back, but I kept my hand wrapped tightly around my phone, like I could hold on to those words. I pressed it against my chest and breathed, lay there and breathed, and reminded myself that, no matter what else happened, I was still loved.

The next couple of days I spent in a self-induced haze. I didn't call Cara, and my mother and I avoided each other as much as possible. It wasn't hard. We were busy getting everything together for my grandmother, and there was enough work to do in different rooms of her house that we could get away with passing each other in hallways with nothing more than a quick hello. She looked uncomfortable whenever she saw me, and I was awkward as hell, but I didn't want to reopen any of it, even if it would make things better. It was too raw right now, and I wasn't sure what was going on with me, but I did think I knew what I could and couldn't handle.

If Gran noticed, she didn't say anything about it. In her bedroom, we surrounded ourselves in an ocean of books. Conversation was always about plot and characters and why she thought certain books were important, or why she loved them so much. I wrote a lot of it down. I felt like I was gathering bits of her life. Even when the books were done and packed away, to go with her or with me, and we'd moved on to packing up the last of her personal things, cleaning out her bedroom closets and her office, we still talked about books. I wasn't surprised our conversation didn't wander much. It was the thing we had in common, and it was safe. But I found myself enjoying it.

I let myself get lost in it, pretended for those few hours every day that there wasn't anything else outside that room, outside the smells of paper and dust and ink. I knew I was escaping, but I didn't care. I wanted a retreat. I wanted time to think. Or not think.

Then it was time for Gran to go. The place was about forty-five minutes away—inconvenient, but worth it for a home that would be comfortable and where the people would treat Gran well. My dad asked me if I wanted to go with them the day they took her. He knew something had happened between me and my mom, but I wasn't sure if he knew exactly what. He wanted to make peace. But the idea of a car ride with my parents, while Gran left her home, struck me as both unbearably uncomfortable and awfully sad. I apologized to Gran about it the day before, but she waved it away. I'd spend some time at home in the morning, and then I'd go over to Gran's house by myself, Zevi would meet me there in the afternoon, and we could work on finishing up the last of emptying the house out.

I waited upstairs in the guest room the day my parents were taking my grandmother. I listened to them moving around downstairs, my father hunting for his keys, my mother telling him right where he'd left them. I could almost picture her with her hand in her purse, checking that she had the right paperwork, her wallet, her phone. I stood with my back against my shut door, eyes closed, and listened and listened, waiting. It was childish and I knew it, but I didn't want to go down there before they left. I didn't want this to be any more awkward than it had to be. I wasn't ready. I didn't know when I would be.

Finally, I heard what I thought was the soft thump of the door closing, then the dull roar of a car starting in the garage. A second later, I crossed to the window, and watched their car leave, moving slowly down the street, pearly and indistinct in the early-morning light.

I took my time after that. Had a long shower. Used up all the hot water, and what did it matter, because there wasn't anyone home but me, and wouldn't be for a few hours at least? They'd have to go and get my grandmother, load up the last of her things and her, and then, after the drive, get her settled. I had all morning to myself.

What I wanted to do, most of all, was go down and play my drums. I stopped for coffee in the kitchen, adding milk and sugar without really stopping to watch what I was doing. My mind was already with my kit.

I had the songs Tuck had sent me. I'd listened to them, over and over, getting familiar with them, diving into them so I could see the spots where I wanted to put different rhythms, different fills. I'd sent Tuck a few suggestions, about where I thought they sounded rough, but mostly that wasn't my area to mess with. I knew drums. That was what I did.

I could have been playing, in the evenings or mornings, over the last few days since I'd set the kit up. But I hadn't. It was loud, true, but more than that, I didn't want my parents to hear me. The thought of it had never really bothered me before, but now I would wonder what they were thinking of it. What my mother was thinking. Whether she was remembering everything I'd said, about how happy it made me. I wondered, when I let myself think about it, whether she'd even tried to understand any of that. If she'd been running it all over and over in her mind like I had, or if she'd dismissed it. I didn't want any of that to bleed over into what I was playing. Maybe for another song. Not for these. These weren't like that.

These songs were all about Bellamy and Tuck being happy. Fast and catchy and with a lot of depth to the sound. When I listened to them, I could picture both of those boys with their partners. Satisfied and content and just fucking pleased with life. Writing songs that made them feel good, that would make people want to get up and move. I wanted that. I wanted to know what it was like. If it made them feel complete. If it was like when we were on stage and we finished a song and the audience roared, so loud sometimes I thought the walls would come down on us. The unbelievable power of that. It must be like that, if it was like anything. And I didn't want to get my anger, or lonely love I had for Tuck, all over that.

I let myself play and play, until I felt like the drumsticks were part of me, and my muscles were moving more from memory than any conscious thought, until I felt like the music was crawling under my skin. It would have been boring for anyone to listen to—it was repetition and mistakes and experiments while I tried to figure out what I wanted to do and exactly how I wanted it to sound. I let myself get lost in it, though, more completely than I'd ever gotten lost in my grandmother's books. Maybe it was the same for her, when she wrote. Maybe it was like she was floating above it all, like she could start to pick out patterns and words and suddenly everything fit and it was the best high ever. That was what drumming was for me. As if I was breathing. As if I could breathe again, when I hadn't even noticed I was short of breath to begin with. I hoped it was the same for her.

After an hour, maybe two—I hadn't checked my phone, and I'd completely lost track of time—I realized that I hadn't eaten anything.

Drumming wasn't always a workout, but I'd been doing enough of it to work up a sweat. I'd have to eat something if I wanted to keep playing.

I grabbed my coffee mug and, with the hum of the songs and the rhythms still flickering through my mind, I went back upstairs. There were a few different things in the fridge, but I wanted something quick. I wanted to get back downstairs, make the most of the time I had. I'd still be here a few more days, until Gran's house was more or less emptied. Who knew if I'd get a chance like this to play again? I slipped a couple of pieces of bread into the toaster and grabbed butter and jam, hesitated for a second, then decided to go all out and have peanut butter too. Why not?

Someone had run the dishwasher, and it hadn't been emptied yet. I flung it open and grabbed a plate, hurrying, then reached back in for a knife. I wasn't looking. The toast had popped up, and I turned my head to see if it was ready, or if I should press the lever down again. I plunged my other hand down, hoping to close my fingers around the knife I'd seen. It was right there.

I must have moved my hand a little to the side when I glanced away, because instead of grabbing the knife, my hand went too far down, and my wrist caught on something sharp. Very sharp.

I yanked my hand back and looked down, but it was too late by then. I'd caught myself on a fork of all things. I stared at the tines, shiny and dark red. I hadn't known a fork could actually stab someone. What a stupid thing.

Then I glanced at my wrist and almost passed out. I'd never been super good with blood. Anyone's blood, in any amount. Tuck would probably laugh his ass off if he could see me swooning in my parents' kitchen over a little cut. Except it didn't really look small. I couldn't actually see the cut, or cuts, because there was so much blood, drizzling out of my arm and onto the clean dishes and the dishwasher door and the floor. Startlingly bright red.

"Fuck." I clamped my other hand over my wrist, but all that did was make the blood squish out around my fingers. A wave of dizziness came over me, and I had to turn away, stare up at the ceiling, and breathe through my mouth for a minute while I got myself under control. I couldn't pass out. Not yet. I couldn't have my parents come in and find me dead on the floor from a fork stabbing. What a fucking idiotic way to go.

I lifted my hand, grabbed for a dishtowel, and slapped that down. I tried to remember what you were supposed to do for something like this. Apply pressure. Right. Except the pressure hurt like a bitch, and the dishtowel was already going spotty and red. Just looking at it was making me woozy. Another wave of dizziness washed over me, a terrible tipping sensation, stronger than before. I stumbled a step, caught myself on the counter, then let myself slide down the cabinet door until I was sitting on the floor. Or sprawled on the floor, but I was still mostly upright. That counted as sitting.

Maybe I needed stitches. I needed something. I wasn't an expert, but collective knowledge assured me that wounds to the wrist were a big no-no, no matter how they were inflicted. I'd need to go to the emergency room. Could I drive? With one hand while I lost blood and tried not to pass out? Maybe not.

I could call my parents. But they were most likely already long on their way, if not already to the place. It would take them at least half an hour to get here. I didn't know if Zevi had gone with them. He might have. Or he might be at Gran's house, two towns over. Or he could be anywhere else.

I could call 911. That was the logical thing, the idea that had been drilled into me since I was a child. In an emergency, call an ambulance. But the idea of it was like a lead weight in my mind. What a fucking fool. Having to call an ambulance because I'd stabbed myself with a goddamn fork.

I took a couple of deep breaths, then carefully peeled my hand away from my wrist. It was hard to tell, but I thought the bleeding was slowing a little. The cloth was dark red in spots, but it didn't look like the spots were growing *that much*.

I had to twist my head to the side and retch a couple of times after, but at least I had a slightly better idea of what I was looking at. Or pointedly *not* looking at anymore.

If Cara was at the studio, she was only one town over, a ten-minute drive at most. She was the closest person, unless I wandered outside and started knocking on neighbors' doors. I didn't want to do that. I didn't want to call the ambulance. Stubbornness and pride and stupidity were all wrapped up in that decision, but my brain was sticking to it. Only if I had to. Only if I couldn't get to the hospital any other way.

I unclamped my hand again and fumbled through my pockets for my phone. When I finally got it to eye level, I had to take a second and wonder why the screen was blurry. Then I realized I'd gotten bloody fingerprints all over it. I shuddered and did my best to forget about it while I searched for Cara's number.

She answered after three rings, and I realized how lucky I was that she'd even heard it ringing.

"Oh good." My voice sounded floaty. "You're not dancing."

"Ava?"

"I need some help." My words were definitely a little mushy. I tried harder to form them, make them sharp off my tongue. I didn't think I'd lost enough blood for that. It must have been the effect the sight and smell were having on me. "I cut myself."

"What?" She sounded sharper, whether I did or not. Her voice seemed closer too, like she'd pressed the phone hard against her ear. "Ava, are you okay?"

"Bleeding pretty bad. I don't think I should drive?" It came out like a question, even though it wasn't one anymore. The sound of my own voice had set off a tiny alarm in the back of my mind. "Can you come get me? I can't . . . I'm alone."

"Are you at home?" she asked, firm and clear. She mumbled, maybe over her shoulder to someone else in the room with her. "Ava. Answer me. Clearly."

I told her I was, told her I was in the kitchen. She made me promise not to move, and then she said, "I'll be there in five minutes. I'm putting you on speakerphone. If I tell you to hang up, do it." I thought I heard her mumble, "I'll call 911," but I wasn't sure.

I didn't know why she'd want me to hang up, but I said okay. Whatever made her get here. I wanted to get off the floor.

It really did only take her five minutes. She talked to me the whole time, a steady stream of assurances and a narration of exactly where she was, how far away she was. If I didn't answer after she said something, she'd prod me until she could hear my voice. By the time she got there, I hadn't looked at my wrist in a while, and I was feeling better. I was also feeling like an idiot, but that couldn't really be helped at this point.

The front door was unlocked, thank god. I probably could have gotten up and let her in—it wasn't my legs that I'd stuck with the fork—but I really didn't want to. She slammed open the door and dashed into the kitchen. She was sweaty, her hair sticking to her forehead, her clothes definitely the ones she'd been dancing in—not something you could really wear outside a studio. She looked flushed and salty and stressed. And beautiful. Shiny and luminous. Like some beacon that had been dropped into my kitchen, and was now calling to me.

"Hey," I said, because I was definitely being super smooth right now.

"Up," she commanded. She crouched in front of me. She stared for a second at the cloth on my arm, pulled my fingers and the corner of the towel back for a second so she could see. Then she pressed both back down and hauled on my good elbow, tugging at me. "Up. We gotta go."

She got an arm around me, and I let her pull me toward the door. I had the presence of mind to make a grab for my keys, sitting in the little decorative bowl, and Cara got the hint. She snatched them up and gave me another push, through the door—she'd left it open, and I was strangely smug at the idea that she'd wanted to get to me so badly that she'd allowed herself to be careless—and out onto the front step. She turned to lock the door behind us, but she didn't let go of me. One hand stayed on my waist, steadying me, and when she was done, she turned back to me, wrapping her arm around me again, pressing her other hand down on my bloody wrist.

"Why did you do that?" she asked as we made our way to her car. She flung the passenger door open and helped me tumble myself inside. Then she closed the door, only giving me the barest glance to make sure I was all the way in, before she dashed around to the driver's side and flung herself into her own seat.

"I wanted a knife," I said after she'd started the car. "They were in the dishwasher. It was faster. Fork got in the way." I was pleased to hear my voice sounding a little steadier. Maybe I was getting over the wooziness.

She spared me the quickest glance as she backed out of the driveway. "What?"

"I cut myself on a fork." I was careful to enunciate each word.

She blinked, and then the stiff, carefully neutral expression she'd been wearing softened and melted a little bit, so I could see the worry and the stress underneath. "Oh. I thought . . ."

She went pink, but it still took me a minute to figure out what she'd been hinting at. I blamed the blood loss. My brain wasn't exactly firing on all cylinders. "You thought I cut myself? Like, on purpose?"

She shrugged uncomfortably, her shoulders hitching up to her ears, and I let out a sharp laugh.

Cara lifted her hand off the wheel, then slapped it back down. "I didn't know! How was I supposed to know?" Her voice was as sharp and humorless as my laugh had been.

"I don't know." I almost wanted to snarl at her, but I didn't have the energy for it. "I wouldn't do that."

She glanced at me again, and she looked angry. "It happens to people, you know. There isn't any shame in it."

"I know there isn't. I didn't mean it to sound . . . I'm not in that sort of place, okay? But . . . I'm sorry." I slumped back against the seat and rested my head on the window. The trees and houses we were passing were a gray-green blur, and I had to close my eyes to stop them from making me nauseous. "There *isn't* any shame in it. But I didn't cut myself." I sighed, even though I hadn't really wanted to. But this seemed like a good place for a sigh. "I mean, I did. But not on purpose. I reached into the dishwasher and managed to cut myself on a goddamn fork. I'm an idiot, okay?"

It took her a long, tense minute to answer, but when she did, her voice was much softer. "I didn't say you were an idiot."

"Just wanted to clarify," I mumbled. I peeked at my wrist through my lashes, keeping my eyes to slits. I didn't really want to see it.

"You should probably keep that elevated," Cara suggested.

I gave a one-shouldered shrug. "I think it's mostly stopped bleeding." I probably could have driven myself after all. I was glad I hadn't called an ambulance.

There was another long silence, still tense, but maybe not quite as tense as before. I dared to open my eyes again, stare out the window.

It had been raining. I hadn't even noticed that, in my determination to get downstairs and play as much as possible. The roads were slick, rain dripping off all the trees, turning the sides of the street into giant mud puddles.

"You scared me," Cara said, drawing my attention back to her. Her voice was even quieter than before, a soft confession. "You sounded really bad on the phone."

I tilted my head so I could see her out of the corner of my eye. "I don't like blood. It makes me dizzy."

"That's why you didn't want to drive yourself."

It wasn't a question, but I answered it anyway. I wanted her to keep talking to me. "Yeah. And I figured the rental car place would make me buy the car if I bled all over it."

She choked out a laugh, and I was stupidly proud of myself. "Thank you," I said after a second, "for coming. I didn't know if you'd . . . I didn't know."

"Of course I came," she replied, very careful not to look at me again. And that was that.

chapter nine

We had to wait in the emergency room, so I guessed I hadn't done nearly as much damage as I'd thought.

Tuck called while Cara and I were waiting. I felt my phone buzzing in my pocket, and when I pulled it out and saw his number, I hesitated.

Cara paused beside me. "Is that something you need to answer?"

I shook my head, because it was only Tuck. But I did want to talk to him. If I had a problem when I was home, if something wasn't right, if I didn't feel good, it was Tuck I called. He was everything that meant comfort and safety to me, and I hadn't thought of it before, but now that he was calling, I wanted to talk to him, even if it was just for a second.

"Answer it," Cara said, a little softer. She leaned forward, into my line of sight. "You kinda look like you want to."

I shrugged, but I hit the button to answer, and pressed the phone to my ear.

"Hey."

"Hi."

"You're calling. You don't usually call."

There was a pause on the other end of the line. "Are you stoned?"

"No?" It probably wasn't a good thing that it had come out as a question. "I'm in the emergency room."

"What?" He went from mildly concerned to panicky, and I could hear the whole transition in his voice. "What happened? Are you okay?"

"Fine, fine. Cut myself. It was an accident. Blood, you know."

I didn't have to explain further than that. Tuck had once snapped a guitar string on stage and bled all over the front of his guitar, and I'd had to run backstage and puke before I could keep playing.

I saw a nurse walking toward us and tipped my head down to talk into the phone. "I gotta go. Did you need me?"

"I just wanted to talk to you. After your text . . ." He trailed off, and I thought he sounded almost nervous. Brave, strong, showy Tuck, who always wanted to stand at the front of the stage. Nervous. It was almost unimaginable.

It took me a minute to remember what text he was talking about too. Then it hit me. "Oh. I can't . . . Not right now."

"I know. You're sure you're okay?"

His voice was so deep and smooth, and I wanted to slip into it and forget where I was. "Yeah. I'm fine."

"Don't do anything crazy, baby. Be safe."

I nodded and hung up. The nurse had reached us and was gesturing for me to follow her. I stood, then glanced back at Cara. She was watching me with an intent expression on her face, and I wondered how much of my conversation she'd heard. I hadn't tried to be too quiet. I wondered what my end of it had sounded like. What my voice sounded like when I talked to Tuck. But she blinked, flashed me a smile, and we followed the nurse together.

When they did finally put the stitches in, there were only three. I hated the feel of the needle in my skin, the tugging sensation there even through the numbing agent they'd given me, but I wanted it to be ten stitches, or fifteen. At least then I'd have an excuse for making all that fuss. I was doubly glad I hadn't called an ambulance, although Cara told me I probably shouldn't have taken the chance of her getting there on time, since I hadn't known how bad it was. The nurse agreed, and I felt like a little kid getting scolded by my parents. By the time the nurse applied the bandage, I wanted to get out of there as fast as possible.

"Are you hungry?" Cara asked me when we were back out in her car. It had started to rain again, just a drizzle, and the drops plunked down on the roof of the car. It made every sound feel close, like we'd been cocooned by the damp.

I thought mournfully about the pieces of toast I'd left on the counter. But then I looked down at my blood-spattered shirt and jeans, and held out my arm to show Cara. It wasn't a lot. It wasn't something I wanted to bring into a restaurant, either, though.

"I'll go in somewhere and we can eat in the car. If you want?"

I hesitated, then nodded.

We went to a little sandwich shop we'd both been to before—it had been years for me, but Cara told me they never really changed. I felt like everything on this side of the country was like that. Old buildings and businesses, plodding along like they always had, and everyone happy about it. Paint peeling and signs going cockeyed, and no one noticed because they'd been staring at it all forever. It wasn't the same, back home. Things changed and shifted and morphed, always looking to do better, be better. I liked that. I liked the surprise. But there was a comfort in biting into the cheese and tomato sandwich Cara brought back to me, and finding the same flavors. The distant familiarity in it.

Cara waited until I'd eaten most of it, and she'd polished off most of her own lunch, before she spoke.

"Were you going to call me again, before you left? If this hadn't happened?" She waved her hand at my arm, making me glance down at the thick Band-Aid the nurse had put on. It still looked pathetically small to me, too small for all the trouble I'd caused. I wanted to cover it up. I wished I were wearing long sleeves. At least I wasn't a gory mess anymore. Or, at least, not quite so much of one.

"Would you have wanted me to?" I didn't want to answer her question with a question—I hated when people did that to me—but it seemed relevant to how I'd answer.

She gazed down at her sandwich, picking a little at the bread. "I don't know."

I took my last bite and found I regretted that it was gone. Who knew when I'd be back here? Maybe never, if I had my way. If I kept avoiding this place like I'd been doing for the past few years. It had been working out so well for me, ignoring all of this. Pretending it wasn't here.

"I wanted to," I said. I had, too. I'd thought about calling and apologizing to her a thousand times, in all those quiet spaces while I worked at my grandmother's house or went out for dinner with Zevi or texted with Micah. But I'd talked myself out of it every time, and it hadn't even taken much effort. "It's not fair to you," I said, even though I'd said it before. "I don't know how you could be okay with it. With any of it."

She did look up at me then. Her chin was still tucked, and she was letting her bangs fall in her eyes, but she was looking at me. Brave girl. I didn't know that I could have held her eyes if she weren't holding mine. "It's only a start for us, Ava. That's all I wanted. A chance to start."

I'd been reaching for my drink, but now I let my hand drop back down to my side. "Even if . . ." I waved my other hand, then winced when the skin tugged at the fresh stitches.

She shrugged. She started gathering up our trash and stuffing it all back into the bag it had come in. "What about what you want, Ava? You're so worried about what's fair to me, what's fair to your band. I know you're going home. I've known that all along. I don't think it makes things impossible." I should have told her, then, about Tuck, but I couldn't make myself do it. What difference did it make? "What about you? Aren't you ever going to be selfish?"

I swallowed, hard. "I've been selfish." I'd always been selfish. Leaving everything so I could have the life I wanted. It had been the most selfish thing I'd ever done.

She only shook her head, though, and buckled her seat belt. I did the same, my movements mechanical, and when I was done, she started the car and drove us back to my house. And we didn't talk any more.

Cara got out with me when we arrived home. I didn't exactly need help—I was more or less fine now, aside from being slightly sore—but I was glad that she didn't just leave. I didn't want our last conversation to be the one we'd had in that parking lot, with bits of our lunch scattered around us. I hadn't known her for very long, and I wouldn't know her for much longer, but I didn't think I'd forget her. I thought, for whatever reason, that she would be something I carried with me for the rest of my life. And I wanted our ending to be decent, at least.

I didn't really get a chance for that, though, because when we walked through the front door, I found that my parents were home and panicking. They were standing in the kitchen, my mother in the middle of shouting at my father. She had salty white tear marks down her cheeks, and her hands were raised like she was going to hit him or throw something. My father saw us first and turned to me, and then she did. In the sudden quiet, I saw what they must have seen when they'd come home: me gone and a rather alarming amount of blood.

I held up my wrist. "It was an accident."

My mother dashed forward, careless of the dried blood she was stepping in and tracking everywhere, and flung her arms around me. I struggled for a second, surprised by the touch, then surrendered into it, and let her hold me up. It felt *good.* Sweet and warm and caring, and not like all those distant-yet-not-distant-enough embraces we'd shared more often than not lately. She hugged me like she'd been afraid, and I held her back because she was my mom and I wanted that child comfort.

I caught Cara from the corner of my eye, shifting nervously from one foot to another. I pulled a little away from my mom. "I cut myself. Three stitches. No big deal." I gestured at Cara. "I called Cara, and she came and took me to the hospital. It was fine," I assured her, hoping it would get through. "You could have called."

"I was about to." She waved her hand, and I saw that her phone was in it. "We only got home a few minutes ago. I was about to dial."

She looked like she was going to start crying again, and I was feeling pretty ragged and raw myself. I really couldn't handle that. I glanced past her, to my father. He was staring at the three of us, his gaze moving too fast between us. He looked stunned and confused and a little dazed. But then his expression cleared and he gestured us toward the living room.

"Why don't you all go and sit, and I'll make some coffee." He ran a hand through his hair and peered around at the kitchen. "Or something," he said, almost under his breath.

My mom nodded and started to tug me toward the living room. Then she looked over my shoulder, to Cara. For a second, I thought she might ask one of us who Cara was, why she was there. She glanced at me, and I thought I saw realization on her face, and I had a second of horrible worry that she'd say something, that she'd make a scene. But she only smiled at Cara, tentative but sincere. "Please. Come in."

Cara hesitated, and I felt myself holding my breath, waiting to see what she'd do. I wanted to nod, or shake my head, or maybe both.

I wanted her to come with me, to follow me into the living room, to show me that she wasn't leaving me yet. And I didn't, because nothing was right between us and I didn't want to make this hurt more by drawing it out.

But in that tiny, sharp second, my phone rang again. My hand went to it automatically, and I checked the caller ID. Tuck. I glanced at Cara, and found her staring at me. My mom was too. But I couldn't not answer, even though it was rude. He'd probably been waiting all this time, and I'd forgotten about him while I was out with Cara.

"Hey," I said into the phone, raising it to my ear as I pushed the button to answer. "I'm fine. We're home."

"What the fuck, Ava," he said, but he sounded relieved. "I thought you'd call me back. I waited. I was worried." I could almost see him shaking his head through the phone.

I felt myself smiling. God, it was good to hear his voice. Aside from that short conversation earlier, I hadn't talked to him, or Bellamy or Micah or Quinn, since I'd sent Tuck the text message telling him I was bi. And I wasn't really nervous about it. I wasn't. But maybe there was a tiny part inside me that, within the relief of finally having that out there, had wanted to hear his voice to make sure everything between us was still the same as it had always been.

"Sorry." I knew I was probably grinning like an idiot, but I couldn't help myself. "You know how I am with blood. It wasn't pretty."

Tuck laughed, and we talked for another minute, him making sure I really was okay, and me assuring him I was. His tone was light and he kept making me laugh. And then he asked me when I was coming home, and he sounded so happy when I told him it wouldn't be long. And I was happy too. I wanted to get back to him, in that second, more than I had all week. I wanted to go home and have things be normal, and his voice on the other end of the phone reminded me that they could be.

It was only a short conversation, but when I hung up, I was smiling and shaking my head at the phone. I raised my eyes and found my mom, my dad, and Cara, all standing there staring at me. I realized how I must look. Flushed and happy. And I realized what I'd said. How my end of the conversation must have sounded. How I'd talked about how glad I was to be going home. How I'd said it wouldn't be long.

The smile slipped off my face, and now my cheeks were burning from embarrassment and not happiness.

"Sorry." I didn't know what else to say. "I just . . . I was glad to talk to him." I felt even worse when I said it. It didn't make anything better.

I glanced at Cara, still standing beside me. Her eyes were wide, and she looked pale and as if she'd gone inside herself. She caught my eye after a second, and her own cheeks burned. And I knew that she knew. I just knew, somehow, that she'd heard something in my voice when I talked to Tuck that had given away how I felt about him.

My mom cleared her throat, and when I focused on her, she smiled at me, slightly, but enough to tell me it was okay. She reached for my hand, then paused and looked past me, to Cara.

Cara smiled, but then she turned to me and shook her head. "I have to get to work."

My mom nodded and stepped back. I took a step toward Cara, uncertain and nervous but wanting to say . . . something. To explain Tuck, or to explain why I hadn't said anything. Cara held up her hand, though, stopping me. She was smiling, but it looked fragile on her face, and I knew she was doing it to try to tell my parents that everything was fine. Doing it to stop me from saying or doing anything, to stop a scene from happening right here in my parents' kitchen.

"Thank you," I said, because I couldn't think of anything else.

She nodded. "Anytime." She took another step forward, touched her hand, the tips of her fingers, to my shoulder. Then she nodded again, smiled at my parents, and let herself out the door.

I tried to act like it was fine. My father made coffee and plied me with cookies, and when I told him I'd clean up the kitchen, he laughed. He patted my hair back from my forehead like I was eight instead of twenty-eight, and told me to lie down and relax. And I found that I was exhausted, undone by the morning and the days before it, everything that I'd kept such a tight rein on for so long coming loose. Maybe his touch was the final straw, but I let go. I stretched out on the couch and flicked on the television, turned it to a nature show, and when he came back and draped a blanket over me, I didn't protest. I let him take care of me.

For a while, I was alone, and I figured he was cleaning the kitchen. I didn't know where my mom had gone, until she came into the room and sat down on the edge of the couch. She'd pulled her hair back, but little tendrils were escaping around her face, and she was flushed. I realized she'd been the one cleaning.

"I think I got most of it." She smiled wryly at me. "What did you do, wave your arm around? You can make such a mess."

I laughed, and that felt almost as good as her hug had earlier, like I was lighter, or like whatever was between us didn't have as much weight anymore.

Then I sobered a little. "I'm sorry." I didn't mean for the kitchen, and she knew it.

"I'm the one who's sorry, Ava." She hesitated, her hand floating between us, and then she rested it on my ankle, a warm, steady grip through the blanket. "I didn't mean to make you feel like you had to hide. I didn't mean to make you feel . . ." She took a deep breath, and for a second, I was horrified that she was going to cry again, but she kept herself under control. "I didn't mean to make you feel like you needed to move all the way across the country just to be yourself. I never wanted that."

Then I was afraid *I'd* be the one to cry. "That's not why." My voice sounded horribly close to breaking. I told myself it was because I was hurt and tired, but I wasn't really sure. "I just didn't want to disappoint you. I couldn't . . ." I couldn't stay here and watch. I knew I could have done everything that I'd done, could have found a band and made music, could have been successful, could have fallen in love, all from here. It wasn't this place that would have held me back. It wasn't that one spot was better for this kind of thing than another, because really what it boiled down to was determination, and I'd always had that. No. It was that I would have felt my parents, my mother, watching me, and I had wanted to go somewhere far enough away that I felt like I was alone. Far enough that I didn't feel the weight of their wants on me, because even when I'd known that what we wanted was different, and that was all right, I'd never been able to reconcile it. Never been able to not feel guilty.

But that was my fault.

"You don't disappoint me." Her voice was firm. She squeezed my ankle. "I'm proud of you. I'm so proud. We both are." She glanced toward the kitchen. We couldn't see into it from here, but I could hear my father whistling and clattering pans around, getting ready to make dinner. I looked to my mother, and she to me. "But I was afraid," she said, her voice not much more than a whisper. "It's so hard. All the things you want. I didn't want you hurt."

"I know." And I did. I hadn't understood it, before, how fear could make her want to keep me from the things I loved. But I'd seen it in her face when I'd walked in the door earlier. She'd been terrified. She hadn't wanted me hurt. I knew I'd probably seen that expression on her face before, as a child or a teenager, but never quite like this. Never as an adult, and never with our last argument so fresh in my mind. It made everything look different. I still didn't like that she'd wanted to keep me safe in that way, swaddle me in things that were easy and boring. But I did get it. Sort of.

She nodded, and I thought she'd say something more about it, but she just passed a hand over her face. When she looked up again, she was calmer, and there was a tiny smile on her face.

"That girl. Cara. Is she . . . ?" She let the question trail off.

I felt like my breath was caught in my chest, and for a second, it was me who was afraid. Afraid that she'd . . . I didn't even know. Question me or tell me I was wrong or that it was only a phase or any of the other cliché things people said. It was stupid, and maybe even irrational, but I couldn't help waiting for it, bracing for something like that. But the smile was still there, and she looked hopeful, like she was trying to bridge a gap, not to create one.

"I met her on the plane," I explained, my words slow at first, but she nodded, and I kept going. "We kept bumping into each other. I . . . I like her."

"She rushed over here and got you to the emergency room," she said, a hint of dry humor creeping into her voice. "I'm inclined to like her too."

And that was that. As simple as that. Her hinted acceptance and her hand on my ankle, and I felt like laughing out loud with the relief of it. Maybe it wasn't everything I'd wanted. Maybe it wasn't close, or perfect. But it was enough, more than enough. More than I'd ever tried to reach for before.

"I think I messed up with her." It tumbled out of me. I had romance problems and I wanted to tell someone. I wanted to tell my mom. "I know I did. When I was on the phone with Tuck. And before that . . ." I trailed off and glanced back up at her.

A tiny grin flickered over her face. "You sounded so happy when you were on the phone with him. I haven't heard you that happy since you got here."

I blinked. "I . . . I miss him."

My mom took a breath. "Does Cara know how you feel about him?"

I must have been *really* obvious on the phone. I shook my head. "She does now."

Her eyebrows drew together. "And him?"

My chest went a little tighter. "He's in love with someone else."

"Oh, sweetie."

I wanted to protest at the endearment, because it made me feel like a toddler. But it also seemed to be able to find its way into the deepest parts of me, like it had sunk right in, and I found myself pulling in breath after breath and trying not to cry.

"You should tell him," my mom said gently. "It'll make you feel better. It'll . . . It'll clear things up, you know?" I nodded, although I wasn't sure if I really agreed with her. "And you should tell Cara."

I shrugged, but then I nodded again, and my mom let it go. She smiled again, soft and kind, and when I drew my legs up, she sat beside me and we watched the strange world of insects unfold in front of us on the TV. We didn't talk any more, except for her to ask why on earth I wanted to know about the mating lives of ants. And although I was sad and hurt and tired and a little bit heartbroken, I felt light and alive and free too.

chapter ten

I didn't call Cara. I thought about it, but it was even more fleeting this time. I texted her that evening, to tell her I was okay, and thank her again, and she wrote back just as formally, and that was that. The end. I told myself to be happy with that, to let it go and let her go and be done with it. But I didn't want to let it. I wanted to do something crazy, like run to her studio and pound on that huge window and tell her I loved her, get her to run outside and into my arms. But those were crazy thoughts, and even if I thought I could love her—and I did; she was sweet, smart, and caring, and if I was going to love anyone, I didn't see why it couldn't be her—I was still in love with Tuck. And I was still leaving at the end of the week. It was as set in stone as a nonrefundable airplane ticket could be.

Instead, the day after, when I'd gotten tired of being waited on and had told my parents in no uncertain terms that I was fine, and they'd grudgingly allowed me to go with them to help finish up at my gran's house, I called Tuck. I'd been thinking about it since my mom had mentioned it. At first I'd dismissed it, because I'd gotten along fine all this time without telling him, hiding it. But then I'd started to wonder if I really had gotten along fine, or if I'd allowed what I felt for him to become a thing that wasn't beautiful or special, but something that ate me up from the inside out, that weighed on me, that I carried around like a chain. And I realized I didn't want that between us. What Tuck and I had *was* special, even if it was never going to be the exact way I wanted it to be, and I didn't want to poison it.

I was standing in Gran's room, the last of the books around me, trying to figure out how to make them go as securely as possible into their boxes. Zevi had already taken most of them to the post office—I'd wanted to do it myself, but my dad had put his foot down on that, and Zevi had agreed with him, overruling me. I had a book in my hand—the one my grandmother had written that she'd said she wanted to take with her. There was a note on the front: *I found another copy. Take this one.* That was it. But I was almost afraid to read the back blurb, because this was the book she'd wanted to keep. It must have meant something special to her, something more, and I wasn't sure if I wanted to know what.

Instead of slipping it into the box, I sat down on the bed—she'd gotten a new one, smaller, to fit in her new room—and, without thinking it over again, pulled my phone out of my pocket and hit the number for Tuck.

He answered right away. He didn't always do that. He knew I'd call back if it was important. But he'd been doing it over the past week. He knew things were shaky for me, even if I hadn't told him all of it. He was going to be there when I needed him.

"Hello, favorite girl," he answered, the smile clear in his voice. He sounded like sunshine and ocean breezes and everything I missed about home, even over the phone. It was like it all came across in his words, the ease of them.

"I'm not your favorite girl," I said, part teasing and part serious. He'd been answering the phone that way for a long time, and he'd never changed it after Lissa. And I'd let it go because hearing it had given me a pure jolt to the heart, a flash of hope and greed that tasted sweet and bitter at the same time.

There was a pause, and then he said, a little more serious, "You're definitely one of them."

I nodded, pressing the phone tighter to my ear. "Tuck." I swallowed and closed my eyes and told myself I had to do this. I had to. This had gone too far for too long, and I couldn't do it anymore. "I love you."

The pause was even longer this time. I looked around my grandmother's room while I waited. There were still some of her things here, things she had decided not to keep, and I was struck again by her lifetime. It was so long. So many years. Did her twenties seem like the distant past now, or were they still fresh in her mind, like they'd happened the day before? When I was her age, would this conversation with Tuck, this week and everything that had happened in it, mean as much to me as they did now? Would it fade into the past and become a watercolor memory? Or would it stick with me, the sights and sounds and feel of it all so present that I could never get rid of it, whether I wanted to or not?

"I love you too," he said finally, but his voice was so low, and the pause had been so long, I knew he knew what I meant. I knew he was trying not to make this happen, as much as I was trying to make it.

"I mean," I said, because I had to have this out, perfectly clear, "I'm in love with you."

There wasn't any pause at all this time. "I know."

"Okay." That was all I needed to hear, really. I just wanted to know that he knew, to have the truth out. That I wasn't hiding it anymore, from him or from me. And my mom had been right. I knew it right away. I was . . . so light. Scared and nervous and worried that I'd screwed everything up. But goddamn if I didn't feel better too.

"Ava." He sounded muffled for a second, and then clearer, like he'd moved into a different part of the house or something. "I love you. But I don't love you like that."

"I know that." I was surprised at how easy it was to say it. It still hurt. It would always hurt a little, I thought, because he would always be there, and I'd always love him, in some way. But I'd been doing this for so long. Holding this inside. Living with this. It was easy to admit how fucked up it was. It was a relief. "And I know you love Lissa. I like her too," I added, because I thought I should. "She's good for you. She's . . . good."

"Yeah." He sounded lighter too, and I wondered how long it had been for him. How long he'd known, and not said anything, because I hadn't been saying anything. How long he'd been pretending, for me, that everything was fine. "Why didn't you ever . . . ask me?" he said. "Why didn't you ever make a move on me?"

"Didn't want to mess the band up." It had been the line I'd fed to myself, over and over, and it wasn't exactly false. But it wasn't all the truth, either. "And I was afraid." That was the truth. The rest of the truth. "Would you . . . Would there ever have been a time for us, Tuck? When it would have worked?"

I could almost hear him shaking his head over the phone. The silence that wasn't quite a silence, because it was so full. "I don't know."

"Yeah. Me either." I didn't. I wished I did. Maybe. Sometimes I thought we'd be so good together, because we were already such excellent friends. I loved Bellamy, and Quinn, and Micah, even, but Tuck was my best friend. The best friend I'd ever had. And all we'd have had to do was make that tiny little shift in our relationship, and it could have been perfect. It should have been easy.

But maybe it wouldn't have been. Maybe we worked as friends but we'd never work quite right as lovers. And maybe if we'd tried, we'd have screwed everything up. I didn't want to lose what we had. It wasn't bold, and it wasn't daring, but it made sense to me. Especially now, now that he'd found Lissa and it was so clear that they were good together.

He sighed, his breath rushing into my ear through the phone speaker. "Why are you telling me this now?" He didn't sound put out. Just curious. Like . . . he wanted to know what was going on with me. And I was suddenly so relieved that I never had tried anything more with him, because this, what we had between us now, was rare and special and it was one of the best things that had ever happened to me.

I was still a little embarrassed to tell him about Cara, though. Talk about messing something up. "I met someone."

"There?"

I nodded. He couldn't see it, but it didn't seem to matter.

"You don't make things easy on yourself, sweetheart, do you?"

I laughed. "Nope."

"A girl?" he asked, then corrected himself. "A woman?"

"Yeah. Cara. She's . . ." I took a deep breath. I could still see Cara dashing through my parents' front door, the panic on her face, my name in her mouth. "You'd like her. Definitely."

"I figured that was why you texted me the other day. I'm happy for you, Ava. I really am."

I sighed and let myself collapse backward onto the bed. The comforter still smelled like my gran's lilac perfume, light and floral and powdery. "I fucked it up."

Tuck barked out a laugh. "Why am I not surprised?"

"I told her I couldn't do it because I was leaving." That was only part of it, but I didn't want to tell him the rest. He might be guessing it anyway. But I didn't want him to feel guilty about something I'd done, and I knew he would if I gave him the opportunity.

He thought about it for a minute. "Is that what you wanted? Did you want a way out?"

"I wanted..." I turned my face into the comforter. "I don't know." My voice was muffled with the fluff of the bedding, but Tuck didn't say anything. "I wanted to be fair. I didn't want to lead her on."

"What about what you want?"

"What about it?" I raised a hand, let it flop back down.

"I mean... Ava, what are you doing? Are you lying down?"

"Yes?"

He laughed again, and it was easy, and this felt easy and the same as it always had. Lighter, maybe, than it had been recently, even. No more secrets. I'd been so afraid. All this time, so afraid, and now that I'd told him, it was like I was floating, like I'd untethered myself, and everything was so much better.

"Okay," he said, a mock command in his voice. "Sit up and listen to me."

I did as he asked, pushing myself up against the remaining pillows. I shrugged when I was ready. "Okay, Captain."

"Did you ask Cara what she thought about that? Or did you decide on your own what was best?"

I didn't want to answer that. It didn't matter. He took my quiet as an admittance of guilt.

"There are ways around you leaving, you know?" His voice was only serious now, gentle and soft. "I know everyone says long-distance doesn't work, but it can. Lissa and I did it, before she went on tour with us last time. It's rough. But it can work. There are ways you could deal with this, if you wanted to." He hesitated, then asked, "Do you want to?"

I thought of Cara again. The way she'd comforted me on the airplane, the steadiness of her hand on my shoulder. How it had felt like she'd grounded me. How she'd come to my rescue the other day, when I was being childish and ridiculous, and all she'd thought about was getting to me.

I thought about the night on the couch in the basement. How she'd felt against me. Warm and sweet and real. How she'd held me after and hadn't asked if I was all right, if everything was okay, but had only wrapped her arms around me like she knew I was scared and lost and happy all at the same time. How much I liked being with her. How much I liked how I felt when she was next to me.

I bit my bottom lip, then let one word out. "Yes." I was almost afraid I was going to cry. I couldn't handle all this gentleness. All this care. It was more abrasive than any rough treatment. "How could I ask her that, though? How could I ask her to do that?" Especially when it wasn't just that. When there was the fact that I'd kept Tuck and everything I felt for him a secret too. I'd gone a ways to fixing that, between him and me. But I didn't know if I could fix it with Cara.

"Ava." He sounded a little exasperated, but mostly he sounded like he wanted to reach through the phone and hug me. Shake some sense into me, then hug me, and I wished he was here to do it. I missed him so much. I couldn't wait to get back to him. "She's a grown woman. She can make her own choices. She can decide what she wants too. The same way you can."

I didn't think it was as simple as that. But Cara had said almost the same thing, hadn't she? And I had said the same thing to my mother, in a roundabout way. I could decide what I wanted for myself. And if I could, Cara could.

"I don't think that option's open anymore," I told him, though.

"Well," he said, and he sounded like he was trying to be comforting but not make it sound like he was being comforting. He knew all the tricks for me. He knew how I worked. I didn't know if I'd ever find anyone who knew me like that, ever again. But maybe I wanted to try. Then he laughed, hard. "Make it open. Do something crazy. Don't leave there without at least talking to her, Ava."

"I . . ."

"If you come back here with that regret all over you, and try to make an album with us, it's going to suck. Don't do it." He softened his tone a little. "Be brave. Don't have regrets. Not over this. Okay?"

I hesitated and then nodded. "Okay." It felt like I was making a promise, and I thought he heard that too.

We talked a little bit more, about normal things—the songs, Micah and Bellamy and Quinn and Lissa, when I was coming home. It wouldn't be long now, and I'd be back where I belonged, with the people I should be with. I'd wanted it so badly, for all the days since I'd gotten here. But now I was only looking forward to it, not rabidly desperate as I'd been. Things had settled. I'd thought I'd have to escape from here, but now I didn't.

We made plans for him and Lissa to pick me up at the airport in a few days, and then we hung up. I was relieved the conversation had ended in such a banal way. I'd been so afraid, all along, that this would change things between us. Change the way he saw me or the way we acted around each other. But, so far, it seemed it hadn't, and I knew I was lucky.

I packed up the last of the books, taped the boxes shut, wrote out my address, and went to see if Zevi was back so we could go. My parents were getting ready to leave, and I met them at the front door. My mother smiled at me, tentative, almost shy. Things *had* changed between us, but I didn't think that was a bad thing at all. It was awkward and uncomfortable, but it was okay. Better than it had been.

Zevi caught up with us, and my parents asked if we wanted to go out—everyone always wanted to feed me while I was here. I agreed, and so did Zevi. I didn't think it was going to be a repeat of the last time we'd all gone out, and it wasn't. We called Zevi's mom, and she met us at the restaurant, and if we weren't all completely comfortable, and if things were still awkward, it was okay. We laughed together and the conversation was fine, and I was glad that we'd done it.

Then, when we were done and we were all standing in the parking lot about to get into our cars, I told my parents I'd be home a little later. My mom gave me a knowing look, and I wanted to explain that I wasn't going to do . . . whatever she thought I was going to do, but I let it drop instead. Zevi hugged me tight, and I made him promise to come out and visit me, so he could see Escaping Indigo, maybe catch us recording. And that was that. It felt, finally, like my time here was done.

I got into my car and drove down the streets that were by this point becoming familiar all over again. In the week since I'd gotten here, the leaves were finally starting to turn, and in the last light, I could pick out gold and deep red amidst the green. I drove past all those old houses and the tiny businesses interspersed haphazardly between them. I let the winding road, so narrow in places it made me nervous, take me through town, into the next, and then I was driving down the main street where Cara's studio was.

I hadn't planned on stopping. I didn't think anyone would be there anymore, late as it was. I just wanted to drive by and put a cap on the end of my time here, make it feel like I'd finished everything, even if it hadn't all gone the way I'd wanted it to. But when I drove down the street, I saw that the studio was still open. It was dark outside by this time, the street only illuminated by the occasional orange bulb in a streetlamp. But pure yellow light was pouring from the big front window of the studio, and as I drove past, I saw Cara there, alone, dancing.

I parked the car and got out. I watched Cara for a second from the other side of the window. I couldn't hear if she was dancing to music, but it didn't matter. The way she moved was like watching music come to life, and for the first time, I wondered how she'd dance if it was one of our songs that she was listening to. I wondered if she'd throw her body higher in the air, if she'd twist and turn and let all the emotion we put into our songs flow through her limbs, out her fingertips and her toes. And I wanted to see it. I wanted to give us a chance to see it.

Instead of standing and waiting for her to see me, this time I pulled the front door open and walked inside. There was a boy standing at the reception desk, and he glanced up when I came in. I could hear music now, faint and indistinct. I cocked my head to the side, trying to figure out what it was, and the boy smirked at me, like he knew exactly what I was doing.

I smiled back at him. "Sorry."

He shook his head. "I love knowing what people are dancing to."

I nodded. "It's cool, right?"

He nodded back, and raised an eyebrow at me.

I gestured toward the big dance space. The door was closed, and we couldn't see in from this angle. "I'm here to talk to Cara. Is that okay?"

"Sure. But wait until her music stops before you go in."

"Okay. Thanks."

I wandered closer to the door. I didn't have to wait long. The song ended, and before another could start up, or before I could lose my nerve, I knocked twice and pulled on the doorknob.

Cara looked like she'd been about to move into a different dance position, but when she saw me, she came back to her feet, lowering her heels so she stood square. She didn't smile or say anything, but she didn't look like she wanted me to leave, either. I took a single step into the room and let the door close behind me.

"Hey."

She gave a little shrug. "Hey."

"I'll go, if you want." It struck me how weird it was for me to always be . . . turning up wherever she was. How this time I'd actually invaded a space that was hers. I didn't want to do that to her. "I shouldn't have . . . I just wanted to . . . see you. I wanted to . . ." I didn't know. I hadn't planned this, not really. Maybe in the back of my mind, because I'd been thinking about what Tuck had said this afternoon. And I knew I wanted something more than that last time I'd seen Cara. Whether anything came of this or not, I didn't want to leave things that way, awkward and sad. I wanted to be able to tell her I was sorry, that she was right, that this could be good. Or, at least, I wanted to be able to say goodbye. It felt important.

She shook her head. "It's fine." She gestured at the bandage on my arm. "How is that?" Another song started then, but it was soft, and I could hear her voice over it.

I shrugged. It pulled sometimes, when I moved it, but it didn't even really hurt anymore. "It's fine," I said, noticing that I was echoing her words. "Cara . . ." I took a deep breath. "I'm sorry. I'm sorry I led you on this whole time—" She looked like she wanted to break in and say something, but I held my hand up. "I know you knew I was leaving. But you thought maybe we could work around that, if we found we liked each other enough. Right?" I waited and, after a tiny pause, she nodded. "I like you. It was good. It could have been good."

She nodded again. She moved so that it almost looked like she was stepping toward me, but I couldn't quite tell. Her bare feet slid so easily across the wood floor. "I know it could have."

"But I didn't give it a chance."

"No."

"And I didn't tell you that I was in love with Tuck."

She flushed. "No. You didn't."

I was the one who stepped forward this time. "I didn't tell anybody." I winced. "Well, I told Zevi. But he's too perceptive for his own good. He'd have figured it out." I waved my hand through the air. "No one knew. It was . . . my secret."

She clasped her hands in front of her, and I watched the fingers of one hand twist through the others. "Not even Tuck?"

"No. I didn't want him to know. I didn't want to wreck what was between us, or the band." I sighed. "I was afraid. And I didn't want to hurt anyone."

She closed her eyes, then opened them. "But you did. Me. And you." She hesitated. "And him?"

I nodded. "I think so. I called him today. I told him. He said he'd known. So he'd been keeping it a secret too."

"So what happens now?" That was definitely a step toward me. We still had most of the room between us, but I was willing to be happy for that one little move.

"Tuck's in love with someone else. So now we see how we are together when we're not keeping secrets." I dropped my eyes to the floor, then made myself look back up. I had to look at her while I said this. "And I try to apologize to you."

She shook her head. "You don't owe me anything. You didn't before. And you don't now."

"I do. I owe myself. I started this thing with you, and I tried to tell myself it didn't matter if I told you anything, because I was leaving and this was never going to be serious." I couldn't meet her eyes now. I moved my gaze over her shoulder, to where I could see the sidewalk through the window, lit up, and the dark beyond. It felt like where that light touched was all of the world. This room and that thin strip of cement, and everything else had vanished. "It was serious. I think . . . it could have been serious. But I didn't want to give it a chance, to see if it could be. But I should have."

I hadn't actually admitted it out loud, that this was bigger and more important than I'd thought it could be. Not to anyone. Not to myself. I'd hedged around it and let the idea play in my mind, but I'd never said it. But it was what I'd wanted. I'd wanted Cara from that first moment when I saw her on the plane, and I'd fallen for her a little more each time we'd met. I didn't know how it happened, how two people built a thing that worked. I'd never had that, not once, and the only other time I'd wanted it, it had been impossible. I didn't know how someone let themself fall in love, how it started. I knew that this thing between me and Cara—whether it was an intense like, or an infatuation, or something that might be love someday—had happened so fast for me. It had crashed over me and tried to drown me, and I hadn't wanted anything more than to let it. I'd wanted to get carried away in her. But it had scared me enough that I'd tried to stop it.

I looked back to Cara. She was sweaty from dancing, her hair a tangle around her face, stuck in places to her forehead. She had tape around her feet and her ankles, and some of her toes looked like she'd completely mashed them, all purple and weird. Her T-shirt had streaks of damp and makeup on it, like she'd wiped her face on it more than a few times. But none of it mattered. Or it made her even more attractive. She worked so hard. She did what she loved. And she was beautiful. Those sharp and soft lines of her body, all intersecting, the strength in her so obvious. I wanted to touch the sleek slope of her neck, the curve of her shoulder, wanted to run my fingers down her arm to her wrist and pull her against me.

"I'm sorry," I said again. "I'm so sorry. And I wish I'd done better. But I was really glad to meet you, Cara."

I hesitated, but she only stood and stared at me, and I figured that was as good as I was going to get. I'd messed up, badly, but I'd gotten to apologize, and I'd gotten to end this in a way that wasn't short and fast and terrible. That was really all I could ask for.

I turned and started to take the couple of steps to the door. The music was still playing, and I was glad I didn't know the song after all, because I didn't think I'd ever be able to listen to whatever it was again without remembering this exact moment, crystal clear and painful.

"Wait."

That single word seemed to have the weird ability to launch my heart right into my throat. I turned, and I was glad I had enough sense left not to trip over my own feet.

Cara was right there behind me, like she'd dashed across the room. I hadn't even heard her move.

"I wanted you to come."

"What?" I felt stupid and stiff, and I was horribly afraid, again, that I was going to cry. I'd be so glad when I could get home and get back to the way things were and stuff wouldn't always be messing with my emotions.

"I wanted you to come. I wanted you to call. I wanted to call you." She threw her hands up in the air. "I wanted to say I was sorry. You tried to tell me that you couldn't do this, that we couldn't let it get serious, that it should be casual, and I didn't listen. I didn't realize you were trying to keep us from getting hurt. And I made it so that we did."

I shook my head. "No, I should have been clear, I should have—"

She raised a hand, cutting me off. Then she laid it, carefully, as if she was afraid I'd tell her not to, on my shoulder. Her fingers skimmed the skin at my collarbone, just visible at the edge of my T-shirt. "I was afraid to call. I was afraid to say I was sorry. And that I got it. But I wanted you to come. I didn't . . . I didn't want you to leave. I didn't want this to be over."

This time, it was like all the air in me had disappeared in one single rush. I couldn't breathe, couldn't remember how, and I wasn't sure I wanted to.

"Are you saying . . . Are you . . .?"

She smiled, shy and nervous, and I realized that maybe she was feeling all the same things I was. I reached out blindly and grabbed for her other hand, and she caught it and squeezed my fingers. "I'm saying let's not have this . . . be over. Let's give it a shot and see what happens."

"Yeah?" I took another step, so we were close enough that I could almost feel her body along mine, the heat of her, and when she let out a tiny laugh, I felt it on my lips.

"Yeah."

I couldn't stop myself from leaning forward and kissing her then. She kissed me back, and I could feel her smiling against my lips. It seemed almost like I could taste the happiness in her, or in me, could sense it in the way she tugged me even closer, closed her hand over the nape of my neck, kissed me hard and deep and without thought.

When we pulled back, we were both grinning like crazy, and I felt so light and wonderful I thought I might float away, if her hands weren't tying me to the ground.

But then I had another thought. "How? How are we going to do this?" Those airplane tickets were starting to feel like a lead weight.

Her own smile faded a little bit, but she shook her head. "I hadn't really thought about that." She sighed but didn't sound unhappy, or even that worried. "I'm not going to say either of us should move across the country or anything drastic like that. We don't even know if this will work." I frowned, and she squeezed my hand again. "Let's just . . . see. I think it might work. Do you?" I nodded, and she smiled again, wide. "Then we should let it. We can do long-distance for a while, until we get a better idea of things. I know it isn't easy. But I still think it might work."

"I think it might." I gave in to what I wanted and pressed my face against the side of her neck, breathed her in. She laughed and wrapped her arms around me, and when I raised my head, she was looking down at me with the best expression on her face. Like she was lucky. Like something so good had happened to her. I'd done that. I'd put that expression on her face.

"And you'd be miserable if you stayed here." Her words were light, but they made me tense. "I can see how much you want to go home."

"I'd do it, though. If you wanted me to." I would, too. I knew it as soon as I said it. "At least until we see whether it's going to work or not. Until we figure something else out." I hoped it would work. Desperately hoped for that. But I was going to at least try to be realistic about this whole thing. Maybe Cara would decide she couldn't stand being with someone who was obsessed with playing drums, or maybe she had a secret love of green beans, my most hated vegetable, and I'd have to make a clean break. Maybe she wouldn't be able to handle it when I toured. Maybe I'd get jealous when she kept long hours at the studio. I hoped not. But I didn't know. That was the whole point. Maybe we'd fit together like the last two pieces of a puzzle, and everything else would be speed bumps in what we had between us.

She moved her hand up, so her fingers ran over my neck, up to my jaw, cupping my face. "I think you would." She nodded, more to herself, I thought, than me. “But let’s not. Let’s not make that the thing that ends this for us. Let’s do long-distance, and if we decide we hate it and can’t be apart, then we can figure something else out.” Her smile went a little shy. “I want to try. And I’m flexible. There are other awesome dance studios. I was coming home from one when I met you, you know? This doesn’t have to be long-distance forever. Just for a little while. Just while we give it a chance.”

It seemed too good to be true, and I wanted to question it, poke holes in it until I knew where all the weak spots were, until I could get a better idea of what could go wrong. But Cara didn’t let me. She dropped our hands, then wrapped her arm around me, and pulled me even closer, until there wasn’t any space between us. She leaned down that inch or two and kissed me again. I felt the press of her fingers against my back, the nearly rough slip of her thumb against my cheek, her lips warm on mine, her bangs tangling with mine. And, in that second, I believed it could work. That we would figure this out and it wouldn’t be long before we were together again. That maybe I could be selfish and want what I wanted, and be with who I wanted, and play drums like I wanted, and all of that was okay.

And then I didn’t feel anything but her, and the two of us together, and the music.

Explore more of the *Escaping Indigo* series:
riptidepublishing.com/titles/series/escaping-indigo

Dear Reader,

Thank you for reading Eli Lang's *Skin Hunger*!

We know your time is precious and you have many, many entertainment options, so it means a lot that you've chosen to spend your time reading. We really hope you enjoyed it.

We'd be honored if you'd consider posting a review—good or bad—on sites like **Amazon, Barnes & Noble, Kobo, Goodreads, Twitter, Facebook, Tumblr,** and your blog or website. We'd also be honored if you told your friends and family about this book. Word of mouth is a book's lifeblood!

For more information on upcoming releases, author interviews, blog tours, contests, giveaways, and more, please sign up for our weekly, spam-free newsletter and visit us around the web:

Newsletter: tinyurl.com/RiptideSignup
Twitter: twitter.com/RiptideBooks
Facebook: facebook.com/RiptidePublishing
Goodreads: tinyurl.com/RiptideOnGoodreads
Tumblr: riptidepublishing.tumblr.com

Thank you so much for Reading the Rainbow!

RiptidePublishing.com

acknowledgments

Many thanks, as always, to my parents. Thanks to May Peterson, for helping me polish this into something lovely. Many thanks to Rain, for looking over this with a careful eye and being wonderful. Thanks to Ryan, for teaching me everything there is to know about music, and for being an all-around incredible person, and Jim, for giving me the basics. Tons of thanks to the Blanketeers, for the immense help, support, and fantastic friendship you offer. And to Cosy, for being the best.

ALSO BY
eli lang

Half

Escaping Indigo series
Escaping Indigo
Scratch Track (coming soon)

ABOUT the author

Eli Lang is a writer and drummer. She's played in rock bands, worked on horse farms, and had jobs in libraries, where she spent most of her time reading every book she could get her hands on. She can fold a nearly perfect paper crane and knows how to tune a snare drum. She still buys stuffed animals because she feels bad if they're left alone in the store, believes cinnamon buns should always be eaten warm, can tell you more than you ever wanted to know about the tardigrade, and has a book collection that's reaching frightening proportions. She lives in Arizona with far too many pets.

Website: leftoversushi.com
Facebook: facebook.com/EliLangAuthor
Twitter: twitter.com/eli__lang
Goodreads: goodreads.com/eli_lang

Enjoy more stories like *Skin Hunger* at RiptidePublishing.com!

Far From Home
ISBN: 978-1-62649-452-7

The Love Song of Sawyer Bell
ISBN: 978-1-62649-579-1

Earn Bonus Bucks!

Earn 1 Bonus Buck for each dollar you spend. Find out how at RiptidePublishing.com/news/bonus-bucks.

Win Free Ebooks for a Year!

Pre-order coming soon titles directly through our site and you'll receive one entry into a drawing for a chance to win free books for a year! Get the details at RiptidePublishing.com/contests.